The Drifter

Essentials Book 1

Jason P. Crawford

JASON P. CRAWFORD

ACKNOWLEDGMENTS

I wish to thank my wife, Cherrie, for her unwavering dedication to our family and to our success.

Also, thank you to Kathy Ree for your editing work. Excellent work!

I owe our amazing cover to Alejandro Palomares Photography, and our cover models: Nathan Vellappally as the Drifter, Tayla Holborow as Liara, and Iker Amaya as Edison. You guys did such a fantastic job!

This book is dedicated to Angelique Gunnels, who got me started writing. Without you, I never would have realized what my true calling in life was. May you walk in the land of dream and mystery.

Finally, thank you, my readers. Without you, I am but a scribe in a room, putting words on paper for no one.

The Drifter by Angelique Gunnels

Ragged at the corner,
With his boots centuries old.
A list'ner
In the shadows where the secrets unfold.
A watcher
On the balcony with a gaze grown cold.
A liar
In the story, where twisted words are told.
A seeker
In the city, where the flesh is sold.
A charmer
In the bedroom, where the lovers hold.
A killer
In the city, with a manner bold.
A digger
In the desert, where the bodies rolled.

PROLOGUE

The Visigoths stood outside the Eternal City, and its gods were nowhere to protect the citizens. Great Mars did not materialize to throw back the invasion; Jupiter did not hurl his lightning from mighty Olympus to deter Alaric and his barbarians. Instead, only men were there to defend the walls of great Rome, and they were afraid.

The legion stationed at the city was massed, arrayed in its characteristic for-

mation. *A hundred years ago, maybe even fifty, this legion would have been made up of ferocious, well-trained and disciplined fighting men. Career soldiers. Now, the legions were local, almost rag-tag. The only thing holding the men of Rome on the battlefield against the barbarian horde was the knowledge that, if they failed, the lives of their wives and children would be forfeit. This courage, the courage of the cornered rat, steadied their spines but did little to still the shaking in their arms or the pounding of their hearts.*

The order came: Charge. Attack. Drive the Visigoths back; protect the Roman citizens. Don't let them through the walls.

The legionnaires advanced in lockstep, the last line of defense of the greatest empire in history, and prepared to face the enemy's charge. Historians would mark this day as one of many that led to the Fall of the Roman Empire. They would be correct, but not for the reasons most would think.

The Salarian gate, a major entrance into Rome, was the main focal point of the attack and the defense. Alaric knew that if he could breach the gate, he would have complete access to the wealth of the Eternal City, the wealth of the Emperors and Senators of old. Over eight hundred years had passed since Rome had been taken by an enemy force, and its years of empire had filled its coffers with the gold and silver of a world taken by conquest. All that stood between Alaric and these riches were a few terrified and ill-prepared Roman legionnaires. He sounded the charge, and the Visigoths, on foot and on horse, thundered toward the Roman formation, bellowing their battle cry.

The formation broke before the barbarians could reach it. The rows split down the middle, clearing a path for someone to pass through. A man, dark-skinned and handsome, bearing armor of flowing, almost liquid, metal. His blade was encrusted with sapphires and rubies that glowed with living fire. He leveled the sword at Alaric.

The Romans had thought that their gods had abandoned them.

But this one had not.

1 - THE DRIFTER

The drifter woke, choking back a scream. He was huddled up in his moth-eaten, weather-worn jacket, cheek pressed on the cold glass of the train's window as it began to decelerate. His seatmate glanced over at the sudden start, then went back to reading a copy of *Forbes* magazine.

The train pulled in to Grand Central Station, New York, at exactly 10:55 a.m. The sky was dark with angry thunderclouds, and the rain fell like gunshots against the roof of the train as it parked. The door slid open to disgorge the passengers, a group of people acting more as one mass than as individuals. The drifter passed through those doors, head down, thinking about his dream.

The same dream again. Why?

A city cop, badge gleaming on his barrel chest, stood in front of the lobby doors, nodding and smiling to residents and visitors who were passing through. The drifter caught his eye for a moment as his feet hit the steps.

"Thanks, Mitch."

Mitch blinked and his eyes widened; his mouth opened, but it was too late to say anything. The drifter kept walking, pulling his worn gray hood up to protect himself from the driving rain as his mind filled with dates, names, facts: Mitch Folton, 32, married, two kids. Passed his Officer's Exam four years ago; it was his second attempt. Worries about his mother, who hasn't spoken to him in a few weeks. Has an appointment at....

The drifter shook his head to clear it of the thoughts which had intruded on his own. These ideas, these *knowings,* often came unbidden to his mind; they could be summoned, when it was necessary, but most of the time the drifter preferred to pretend that they weren't there at all.

Squinting through the downpour, he stepped into a crosswalk guarded by a red, forbidding hand. As his feet touched the painted pavement, the hand vanished, replaced by a jovial green walking man. He didn't bother to look up, even as several cars in the cross-traffic screeched to a sudden halt, the drivers reacting to the sudden change as the lights facing them went from green to red, skipping yellow entirely. The drifter was unconcerned; his lights were always green when he stepped into the street. He knew this.

He did not know why.

Men and women in business suits and dresses covered their heads with raincoats and umbrellas as the crowd surged to cross the street. Some sought an escape from the blustery April storm, while others had a definite destination in mind or an appointment to make. The drifter passed through the crowd, making no eye contact; the pedestrians recoiled from him, either repulsed by his torn clothes and soleless boots or afraid of his swarthy skin and long dark hair, reminiscent of a wound whose scar still throbbed just beneath the city's skin.

The drifter registered these feelings of fear and revulsion, and shrugged. The judgment of others rarely bothered him; there was always a vague impression in his mind that these people were *blind*, were *deaf*, were crippled in some way that he couldn't place, that he didn't understand.

"I don't understand myself." He ran one hand through his hair, then pulled his hood back up. "Why should I understand any of them?"

Just on the edge of the street, one of the people walking in front of the drifter dropped something; the drifter tried to call out, but the gentleman was already lost in the crowd, invisible in the masses. The drifter knelt down, picked up what the man had dropped. A wallet. Leather, well-made, and, as a moment's examination revealed, packed with cash and credit cards behind the pictures of family and friends. The drifter smiled and shook his head, taking a moment to reach out to the thrumming he always felt just beneath his awareness.

Then he threw the wallet into the street.

It traveled in a slow, high arc. A gust of wind caught it, and it spun like a baby helicopter's rotor. A city garbage truck, big and green, caught the wallet on its windshield as it drove by.

"What the hell?" The driver's eyes widened, but before he could react, his wipers switched themselves on, brushing the wallet off the truck and sending it skidding back onto the sidewalk. The drifter paused, closing his dark brown eyes, waiting, just for a moment. Then it came.

The amazed laugh, the sound that someone makes when they can't explain their good fortune; the owner of the wallet was grinning, regaling complete strangers with the tale of how he hadn't even known he had lost it, but it came flying out of nowhere and landed at his feet. God must have been looking out for him, he said.

Not exactly. The drifter chuckled and shook his head as he went on his way...whichever way that was.

He sat down under the brown awning of a barber shop. Fat raindrops streaming down the red and white barber pole in front of the store caught the man's attention and drew his weary gaze. He closed his eyes for a moment, listening to the drumming of the drops on the street and the awning above him, letting the sound of the rain soothe his weary soul.

"Commander! The enemy troops are surrounding the city; they have begun setting up their siege equipment. What are your orders, my lord?"

The drifter's eyes flew open. Before him, at attention, stood a young man, European, wearing some sort of military uniform, but archaic, leather and metal. He bore a sword and dagger on his belt, and the drifter could hear the sounds of panicking citizens below him.

"What?" The drifter's gaze darted around, unable to settle. He was on a crenellated stone wall. He could see archers, men with bows loosing arrows at unseen targets. A glance over the wall showed a massed force preparing to fire on the city with catapults.

"We are outnumbered fifty to one, my lord." The officer removed his helmet, kneeling down beside the drifter. "We need your orders. Do we fight or do we flee? We have little time before the enemy will have cut off our escape."

"No." He stared at the officer, then covered his face with his hands, closing his eyes and beginning to rock back and forth. "No, not again. Not now. This isn't really happening. I'm dreaming again. I'm not here. Not here. Wake up. Wake up." The drifter went on in this vein for what felt like hours before he felt a tap on his shoulder. His head snapped up and his eyes searched out the source.

As he refocused, the drifter found a friendly, wrinkled Asian face with warm brown eyes smiling down at him. The drifter stared at him for several seconds; the strange hallucinations came at irregular intervals and it was often difficult to tell if one had ended or simply changed. The city smells--gasoline, refuse, and concrete--soothed him, cradled him in their familiar embrace.

"You all right there, son?"

I'm back. The drifter let out his breath in a great rush. *I made it home. I'm back.*

"Son?"

"No." The drifter shook his head, waved off the man's concern. "I mean, yes, yes, I'm fine." The two pairs of eyes met and held each other for a moment. "Thanks."

"Do you need anything? Are you hungry?"

"No." He narrowed his eyes and cocked his head. *Wait...something's not right.*

"I hope that you were not having a nightmare." The man pursed his lips. "You seemed to be in...distress while you were sleeping."

The drifter nodded. "I was, in fact. Thank you for waking me."

He listened to himself speak, and to the friendly gentleman.

Goddamn it.

The friendly gentleman was speaking Japanese.

So was he.

He looked around; he was still amongst skyscrapers, but the crowds had changed. Billboards now showed *katakana* and *kanji* instead of English letters. The models were different, and the buildings seemed to crowd in on each other even more than back in New York.

As he thought the question, *Where am I?*, the answer came. *Tokyo.*

He was in Tokyo.

"Not again." He picked his body up off the ground and brushed himself off. He bowed to the friendly gentleman, who returned the courtesy, and then started to walk the streets of the capital city of Japan. Much as New York had become, Tokyo was a strange amalgam of cultures, and the drifter found himself falling into familiar customs and greetings within moments; the language of passers-by was as clear to him as if he had been born to it, as were the gestures of politeness, of rudeness, and the subtext beneath each of them. Music videos blared at him from shop windows as he passed, and a variety of vending machines offered every product from condoms to coffee.

Two sugars would be nice. The drifter's thought flowed out, almost a command, as he approached a coffee dispenser. The vending machine complied, providing a steaming Styrofoam cup of liquid caffeine and two packets of sugar. The drifter pocketed the remains of the sugar packets and sipped the coffee as he walked. The night was lit by neon lights and 24-hour shops, but the lack of rain was a welcome change.

The drifter passed by an alleyway and saw several of his "compatriots," men and women huddled together in sleeping bags, lying on the litter-spattered ground. Two men were counting out coins and bills; one of them exclaiming, nudging his partner as he brandished an American five-dollar note.

His friend took the cash and shoved it down his sock, laughing.

The drifter searched out an abandoned doorway – the building looked like it had once been a video game arcade, perhaps – and curled up in it. City police passed him, looking for homeless trespassers.

They did not see him.

The drifter closed his eyes and, as he began to drift into sleep, he had one thought, one prayer: *Please let me sleep without any dreams. For once. Please.*

~~~

The dark god, defender of the Eternal City, stood before the barbarians. He was clad in the arms and armaments of his station: metals undiscovered by mankind, twisted and
~~~

smelted using techniques the Romans would swear must have come from Vulcan himself. He walked forward, his sword leveled in challenge toward the Visigoth king, and the horde hesitated; they had rarely seen one with the courage to face their leader in single combat, and they had never borne witness to a man, a god, such as this walking the Earth.

The Roman soldiers, fearful and cowering only a few moments ago, now whispered gossip like tired old women and men in sunlit plazas. Who is this? I thought that he was only a story...

The god paid them no attention. He knew what had to be done. In order for his city to survive, the invaders must be driven off, slaughtered if necessary. His sword burned with pure white flame, coruscating down the blade in pulses and rivulets of phosphorescence. His visor came down, hiding his eyes from the enemy.

The first of the enemy soldiers broke the trance they had been held in and with a bellowing war cry, launched their attack, goading their horses into a charge and aiming their spears at their solitary foe. The god stood, watching the attack come, his attitude patient, waiting.

The spear tips slammed into the smooth metal of the god's armor. Light flowed up the shaft, causing the weapons to glow like the sun seen through a looking-glass. The horses recoiled, their screams splitting the air and their riders tumbling down, grabbing at their eyes in pain, some going so far as to grab their daggers and dig out their own in order to stop the burning within them.

Cheers erupted from the Roman forces, and the Visigoths fell back several steps on seeing the fate of their comrades. The god began to advance once more, his mouth and eyes grim beneath the helmet he wore. He marched toward Alaric, whose brave words of encouragement to his men were betrayed by the fear writ upon his face.

Then the god felt the cold embrace of Death clasp at his heart.

~~~

The drifter opened his eyes, breathing hard, the sweat streaming off his forehead. A
~~~

gorgeous sunrise was dawning; the sunlight played on the sparkling surfaces of the domed, spiraling roofs. He took a moment to get his bearings, then he groaned.

Goddamn it. Moscow.

The air was crisp and cooler here, and the morning fog clung close to the ground. Already, businessmen and women were heading to their workplaces, bundled in jackets, shading their eyes against the morning sun. The drifter shook the dew off of himself, then stood, looking around to find the nearest bus station.

Last time I was here, I ended up in a brothel. He shook his head at the memory. In the same room had been a young girl, fifteen or so, and she had been shivering. The drifter had padded over to her bed to cover her with one of the thin blankets from the floor.

That was when the burly, drunk Russian barged in. One look told the inebriated man all he needed to know – the drifter was about to molest his daughter. Despite the drifter's best attempts to convince him otherwise, that discussion had ended with a broken nose for the drifter and a shattered arm for the Russian.

The drifter laughed as he watched the bus pulling toward the stop. The daughter had slept through the whole thing, too. Poor girl.

For just a moment, a deep but quavering voice seemed to whisper in the drifter's ear

(*please don't go*)

but he shook his head and pulled himself up the stairs onto the city bus. He sat near the front and closed his eyes, trying to concentrate, forge a deeper connection to that strange *something*. ...

Not feeling tired. Should be able to do it. Nothing happened. *Concentrate, damn it!*

The bus pulled to a sudden stop, causing unprepared riders to jerk forward in their seats. The passengers murmured, looking out the windows, some of the voices rising in alarm. The drifter did not look up, simply flipped himself out of the seat and headed to the door.

<<What the?>> The bus driver tried to grab him, but the drifter ignored the man as the bus door swung open of its own accord. The air that rushed in was moist and much warmer than the Russian chill trapped in the bus, and the murmurs turned to gasps as the collected

passengers saw Japanese faces looking at their transport. The driver shut the door and sped off.

When the bus left the station, it would be back where it belonged. The drifter knew this. He did not know why.

Not that it matters. I just need to find somewhere to hide for a bit. Get control of myself. Calm down. He pulled up his hood, thrust his hands into his pockets, and hunched his shoulders as he walked, hoping to project an air of "leave me alone."

Goddamn Robert Louis Stevenson had it right. Let your control slip for just a second...and you're Mr. Hyde again. Got to be more careful or she could find me again.

<<Excuse me, sir?>>

The drifter stopped in his march toward another hiding place and turned toward the voice. At first he did not see the source. Then he looked down.

A young Japanese boy with bright eyes was standing before him, looking up at him. His hands were holding a steaming bowl of chazuke, rice topped with pickles and covered in hot broth. He smiled at the drifter, then glanced backward. The drifter followed his gaze to see two adults, probably the boy's parents, nodding to him and smiling from the door of a nearby restaurant. The boy turned back.

<<I...I saw you walking, and I thought you looked hungry...so I brought you this.>> The boy bowed, holding the hot dish in front of him; after a moment's hesitation, the drifter returned the bow and took the bowl from him.

And yet again. He brought the bowl to his face and inhaled the rich, savory smell. *Simple kindnesses from a child. Would that we were all children.* A smile began to creep across his lips, and words of thanks formed in his mouth...and then his heart quickened with fear.

SHE was coming.

<<What's wrong?>> The drifter paid no heed to the child's question. Like an animal sensing danger, he did what instinct told him to do – he fled.

Move quickly. He raced down busy Tokyo streets. *Blend in.*

Hide. He tore down alleyways, bumping into pedestrians, ignoring cries of indignation.

Hide. Into a central plaza, teeming with people moving in herds, back and forth. *Hide.*

2 – THE DARK WOMAN

The drifter curled up next to a soda vending machine as she arrived. She emanated presence, a palpable feeling of power as she strode down the Tokyo sidewalk, arriving from Somewhere Else (wherever that might be). The city residents gave her a wide berth, like prey animals avoiding a predator in their midst. Her sleek black dress clung to her form and complemented her smooth, lightly-tanned skin.

The Woman's nostrils flared as she paused on the other side of the vending machine. Her golden eyes narrowed, as if trying to pinpoint something almost seen in the distance.

To the passers-by, she was a beautiful foreigner who exuded a powerful charisma.

To the drifter, she was a hawk and he a mouse.

Hide. He put his hands on his head, a futile gesture. *I'm not here. Go. Go, please. Please go.*

The Woman scanned slowly from side to side, a look of concentration on her face. She licked her lips as if tasting the air on them, and her gaze fell on the soda machine.

A pedestrian, talking on his cell phone, bumped into the Woman. As he bowed, her glare burned holes through his skull. As he rose, however, her look of fury transformed into a smile...but a smile that chilled the drifter's blood, even from his hiding place.

<<I am sorry, miss,>> The businessman who had collided with her bowed again.

<<Not as sorry as you will be, my friend,>> Her voice was susurrant, soft.

As the gentleman looked up at her in surprise, she brushed his cheek with her fingertip. A spark of static electricity flew between them.

<<This is for throwing me off my hunt, wormling,>>

The businessman blinked once, twice, and she was gone without a trace. He looked about in confusion for a moment, then shook his head and shrugged. He hurried off, muttering to himself as he walked.

What the drifter saw, however, was far from rational. On the man's cheek, where the Woman had touched him, was a mark, seared into his spirit like a brand, a sigil writhing with ancient evil and malice.

The *athalaxa*.

The cursed sign of hatred and misfortune, which would drive this man into insanity before allowing his death. He would be plagued like the Biblical Job, losing all that he held dear – his love, his money, his health – until he was unable to bear what his life had become.

This was his fate now. The drifter knew this.

He did not know why.

But he *did* know that the man did not deserve this.

The drifter stood and raced after the accursed businessman, reaching for the other man's head with grasping hands.

<<What!? Who...>>

The drifter gripped the other's head between his palms and touched their foreheads together, despite the other's struggling, despite the people who tried to pull him off, bystanders who didn't *understand*, those coming to the businessman's aid. Holding their brows together, he began an incantation in a language that he knew came from his deepest soul.

<<Begone, sign of vengeance; your wrath is spent. Begone, sign of hatred; your power is stilled. Begone, poisonous sigil; your rage is void and I cast you out!>>

As the drifter intoned these words, reciting them and pouring himself into them as might a man on his deathbed recite long-forgotten prayers, the streetlamps flickered and the syllables reverberated from the walls nearby, echoing as if the two of them were in an empty cavern.

For a moment, the fog that shrouded the drifter's past thinned; it seemed as if a gust of wind could clear the webs and reveal the secrets to the mysteries he lived with each day. For a moment, the drifter felt like a part of something greater, as if he were *more* than what he had become.

Then it was gone, and the drifter was just the drifter, falling over from exhaustion as the businessman fled in fear. The others who had come to help looked confused and concerned, walking away muttering about the "crazy homeless guy." The drifter picked himself up and hobbled over to a nearby wall, leaning against it for support.

The *athalaxa* was gone. The man was safe; he would never know how close he came to utter destruction, of drawing the wrath of powers beyond his comprehension.

What the hell am I talking about? the drifter thought, an edge of panic in his mind. *How do I know these things? Who was she?*

Who am I?

For the first time in a long, long time

(*how long*)

the drifter felt more than an idle, passing curiosity about that question; he felt more than an acceptance of the circumstances of his present. He felt concerned for his future; this woman, this dark Woman, wanted him and wasn't giving up. Every time she showed up, she seemed to come closer and closer to finding him. His safety, his life, depended on figuring out who she was and what she wanted from him.

But that's not all, is it? In the deepest part of his gut, where survival was less important than

(*than what? What is more important than survival? I don't know*) he was afraid...and more.

The Woman felt...wrong. Alongside the ever-present fear was a deep-seated revulsion, as if a part of his soul had been warped inside-out, chewed up, spat out again, and plastered on a wall as a display. The Woman violated his very being in some way.

Why? What's wrong with her? With me? How do I know her?

The drifter was sure of one thing – finding out where the Woman came from and what She wanted would involve piercing the shroud that obscured his past memories, the memories he had lost.

The dreams. The dreams of someone else's life, a life he didn't recognize. Or one he had blocked out, perhaps. He couldn't remember. And the prospect of remembering scared him most of all.

Why had he forgotten in the first place? It surely wasn't benign; if a man's past had an evil Woman who could appear and disappear in an instant, and curse others to Hell on Earth...

As the drifter walked toward the nearby subway station, he cast his mind as far back as his memories would take him, back to waking up in the New York gutter six months ago, covered in street litter. Plagued with a rampaging headache, he had stumbled to his feet and managed to make his way to a soup kitchen, where he had been cared for by kind city volunteers, the first of many small kindnesses that he had vowed to repay. Before that...he simply didn't know. The memories weren't vague, or fogged; it seemed as if parts of his mind were just *gone*, as if they had never been.

Who could have done such a thing? He stepped through the subway doors, standing amongst the staid Japanese travelers who did their best to ignore him, as they did everyone else on the subway who they did not know.

The subway pulled in to its next station, and the drifter exited the underground train, leaving the Land of the Rising Sun and stepping back into the American population center known by many as the Big Apple. Once again, this did not surprise him, although this time he was aware that he was not surprised. He sighed with relief and his shoulders slumped when his furtive glances did not reveal any traces of the Woman.

Quickly. I must move quickly, before she finds me again. Traveling too much draws her attention.

Walking as fast as he could without attracting notice, the drifter approached the turnstile awaiting his ticket card. The turnstile beeped and ushered him through as he approached, a fact which failed to pique the curiosity of the nearby security guard; a single man walking through a turnstile was not nearly as interesting as the fantasy world of the comic the guard was reading. The drifter pushed past the crowds in the stairwell and hurried to ground level. The rain had stopped, leaving children jumping in puddles on the street and New Yorkers shaking off their umbrellas to stow them away in little satchels.

The drifter jogged to the nearest bus stop, ignoring the sidelong glances and shifting movement of others away from him as he sat down.

"Mister, why are your eyes glowing like that?"

The drifter looked over to see a little girl with black hair and a yellow dress. She spoke with the clear, ringing tones of a child who has not yet learned fear, and she was gazing at him with a look of wonder.

"Sarah, we don't talk to strangers!" The girl's mother was curling in a protective stance, not even looking in the drifter's direction as she reprimanded her daughter.

"No, Mama! Look! His eyes are glowing, just like an angel on TV!" Sarah tugged, trying to look more closely even as her mother led her away.

The drifter watched her go, and then his gaze fell on one of the rain puddles, and his reflection therein. *What had she seen?*

He looked into his own eyes.

And fell into them.

3 – THE SHADOW LISTENER

The man known as Medina, which, in the tongue of the Quran means "city," finished his slow, luxuriant morning shave, still trying to shake off the tendrils of his nightmare from the night before. He had dreamt, again, of fallen Rome and the death of its champion. He turned away from the mirror and called to his servants for food and clothes. The servants brought fruits which came from all over the Holy Land

– grapes, figs, dates – and a rice dish cooked with lamb, which Medina found delicious.

He had just finished his repast when a messenger knocked at the door.

"My Lord Medina." The messenger held his hands folded and kept his eyes averted. "Salah al-Din needs to speak with you in his chambers at once."

Medina nodded and scratched at what was left of his beard. "Inform Al-Nasser that I will attend him at once." He turned away from the messenger. "You may leave now." The messenger bowed low and scurried away.

Medina dressed himself in luxurious blue and gold silks and prepared for his audience with the Sultan. As he readied himself, he began to hear the voices again, voices from other places, other peoples, murmuring at the edge of his consciousness. As he generally did, Medina shut them out, pushing them away until there was once again silence in his mind. Not for the first time, he wondered why he could hear these whispers when no one else could, even if they were standing with him when the voices started to speak. What was it that made him so different?

Medina powdered himself with orange- and vanilla-scented incenses and left his chambers, heading toward the center of the palace; functionaries and servants stepped out of his path and murmured apologies for the perceived inconveniences they had caused him. In short order, he had arrived at the understated doors he had been searching for. Medina drew a deep breath and pulled himself up, before he pushed open the doors leading to the private study of the Sultan himself.

Salah al-Din was seated behind a tall desk of cedar, which was turned to the right from the doorway. He had in his hands a gloriously-illuminated copy of the Quran, the holy book of Islam, and sunlight streamed through the well-placed windows and caught the dust dancing in the slight breezes which swirled over the book.

Medina rapped on the doorframe, and the Sultan looked up at the sound. A smile broke his weathered but proud face, a reflection of the glory which had earned him the title of "Al-Nasser," the Eagle.

"Come in, my friend!" Salah al-Din raised one hand in welcome, placing a ribbon bookmark between the pages of his Quran with the other before stowing it on one of the many bookshelves surrounding his desk. Medina approached and bowed, but the Sultan rose, came around the desk, and embraced him.

"No, my brother. I owe you much, too much to have you bow to me this way. Come, we have important things to discuss, you and I." Salah al-Din gestured for Medina to join him at a grand table adjoining the study; upon the table was a hand-drawn map of the Holy Land, with the cities of Acre, Tyre, and Jerusalem, among others, marked clearly. The Sultan gestured to the area on the map surrounding Jerusalem, where he had placed several models depicting his forces, preparing to assault the high walls of the sacred city.

Medina followed his lord. His stomach churned and he rubbed his hand across it. *I wish I could explain to him. I wish that he would just understand.* He shook his head, but his host did not notice his discomfort.

"Thanks to the blessings of Allah, through your knowledge of His divine will, our war against the Franks has gone very well, and we are prepared to take the holy city of Jerusalem.

Allah has sent you to guide us to victory, and so you have."

Medina nodded, but his thoughts were not so pleasant. *I am not a prophet, nor a holy man. God has nothing to do with this.*

He himself had appeared from nowhere only a few years ago, in Damascus, when Salah al-Din was called to assist the ruler there, a child under the authority of his regents. Medina had felt drawn to the Muslim warrior in some way, as if there were a missing piece of his past connected to him. Medina had no idea where he had come from before waking up that day in Damascus. Even his name was simply the first word to come to his mind when it was asked of him.

The Sultan continued: "By the blessings of Allah you have come." He strolled around his office, stroking his long, greying beard. "And by the blessings of Allah we shall achieve victory once more!"

Medina bowed to his lord. "What would you ask of me, my Sultan?"

Salah al-Din paused, looked down for a moment, then met Medina's eye. "I need you to pray to Allah, and ask him what our enemy is planning." He hesitated a moment. "Then I need you to ask for His help to throw open the gates of Jerusalem. We will not take the city against His will; it is His City, and it is not for Man to control it against His desires."

"It shall be as you say, my Lord. I shall...commune with Allah and pray that what you have asked may be granted." Medina bowed once more, hiding his grimace of displeasure. "Peace be upon you, Al-Nasser."

"And upon you, Medina. Go with Allah."

Eyes down, Medina took his leave, returning through the palace to his chambers, hurrying on his way with his thoughts racing. What the Sultan had asked of him was simple enough for him to do – he had done just this same thing many times before, under Salah al-Din's request – but he always felt like he was lying to his lord. Salah al-Din believed that his servant invoked the powers of Almighty God to accomplish his miracles.

He did not.

Medina was not sure how he was able to do the things that he could – why he was able to move from city to city by thought alone or hear what others were planning in distant places.

Why he could walk up to locked gates and ask them to open...and they would, without hesitation.

Why the cities would talk to him.

Why he could hear the various parts of the towns — the buildings, the streets, the public places — clamoring for his attention. Why they called him by name, as if they *knew* him, wanted something from him.

Most of the time, Medina did his best to ignore the voices, to hide from them. It usually worked.

When Salah al-Din asked, however, he was forced to open his eyes, to remove his blinders...and *listen*.

Arriving at his chambers again, Medina locked his doors and closed the curtains, shrouding his opulent room in twilight colors. He lay himself down on a hammock stretched between two marble pillars, and closed his eyes.

Eyes shut on the outside, he opened them on the inside.

Medina's mind was suddenly crowded with feelings, images, names, and thoughts from...other places, some near and some far:

Acre, London, Hangzhou, Toledo, the voices came from all these places and more, in a multitude of languages. Medina knew none of these languages, yet he understood every one. Beneath the buzzing of conversation between men and women around the world, there was a deeper, vibrating tone which called to him, pulling him toward it with a current of base instinct and power, inhuman but recognizable; it came not from the people of London, but from *LONDON;* not the Emperor hiding in Hangzhou, but *HANGZHOU* itself. Every city was known to him, every major human settlement touched his mind...and they were all calling for their absent father.

It was a plaintive cry, as if they were lost sheep; the cities beckoned him, searched for him, with powerful determination but a child's need. The need washed over Medina and the calling he heard

(come where are you come home come home)

was just beyond understanding. Medina did not know how this could be; did not know cities, *cities,* could miss someone, could *need* someone, nor how he was connected to them.

For the moment, however, it did not matter; there were important tasks at hand. Medina mustered his will, keeping himself hidden from the whirlwind of power he felt surrounding him.

"Jerusalem."

There was a moment of fear, as always, that *JERUSALEM* had seen him, sensed him somehow....and then it was gone, and Medina felt the breeze on his face. He opened his eyes once again.

Medina stood in the center of the glorious City of Jerusalem, home of God on Earth. Crusaders were evident in their military garb, crucifixes apparent in their jewelry and their heraldry. They patrolled the walls and the streets, but they were fewer in number than one might expect; the King of Jerusalem had been defeated some days ago, his armies destroyed and he himself captured. Still, men and women prepared for the oncoming battle, moving and storing supplies in preparation for a siege – here, a woman filled water barrels and placed buckets for dousing flames; there, a group of boys, none older than fourteen, practiced the use of a sword under the guidance of a youth no more than five years their elder. City folk worked on preparing the war machines for combat, hauling chunks of masonry for the catapults and trebuchets. The entire walled city was bustling with activity.

Medina took a deep breath and gathered himself, preparing to, once again, shut out the voices, to force them out so that he could marshal his own thoughts. Without warning, Medina's mind was flooded with fear, the fear that a rabbit must feel when it sees the wolf stalking it. There was something else, too...a strange thought

(Clip-clop, the footsteps come.

Damnation rides before them.)

that he knew but could not place. His eyes darted around in panic; the streets were empty, somehow...where had the people gone? Instead of the bustle of war preparations, he heard only one sound: a horse's hoofbeats.

Clip-clop. Clip-clop.

Run! Every instinct told him to flee, but he was frozen in fear, like a bird before a cobra, caught in the hypnotizing aura of terror.

Around the corner she came, on a magnificent white charger and clad in shining maille.

Old men would tell stories about her, this woman who outshone any knight; they would tell of a beauty which belied her fierce strength and nobility.

Anyone who looked into her eyes, however, would know that, despite her comeliness, despite her flowing dark hair and radiant smile, there was no nobility to be found in her soul. Her eyes burned with a deep, slow fire that threatened to consume the onlooker.

To stare into this woman's eyes was to see Vengeance, to see all of the wrongs one had done revisited upon them.

Those same eyes were smiling at Medina, locked onto his, and he saw only a void, an emptiness, awaiting him.

"Hello, Oreth." The Dark Woman's smile was sharp and cold. "It's been a very long time."

Medina was speechless – he did not know what to say, and he was not sure that he could say it even if he knew. His mind rebelled against the evidence of his senses...insisted that there was something terribly *wrong* within her and that he was in danger.

He still could not bring himself to move.

"Nothing to say, dearest? It's too bad." The Woman dismounted from her horse and ambled toward him.

"Wh-wh-who are you?" Fear was clouding his vision; he took a step back, pressing himself against a marble statue of a soldier in the courtyard.

"Come now, Oreth." Her voice was mocking, and her eyes burned into his flesh. "You don't expect me to fall for that, do you? Azrael *is* curious, you know, about how you escaped him." Her lips stretched into a gruesome, sadistic smile. "Maybe I'll even let you live long enough to tell him."

Medina shook his head. "Azrael? Escaped? I don't know what you're talking about!" His words were shrill, panicked; he was on the verge of tears.

The Woman stopped, genuine surprise filling her face. "You...you...don't remember? You've forgotten? Everything?" Her eyes dipped, flitting back and forth on the ground, looking at nothing. They gleamed, as if she was about to cry, and then her features hardened with rage.

"No." She cut the air with her hand. "You will not have that, that...escape! You will not forget how you wronged me when I trusted you." Her eyes blazed with hatred and anger, and her words climbed to a crescendo as she approached him, the force of her presence driving him to his knees. She reached out and took his head in her hands, pulling him to her level. "You will not go into the embrace of the Eternal having forgotten my name, Oreth! I shall not allow it!" She was crying, tears mixing with the rage, anger coursing down her face as she held one of her hands before Medina's face, fingers crackling with some dark, eldritch power.

"No, please no, I don't know...what..." Fear robbed him of thought and will. As his doom approached him, he forgot about the voices, about the barriers he constantly held in place to keep them from reaching him. Without his attention, the walls he had erected to keep himself hidden fell.

And *JERUSALEM* found him.

(*FATHER!*)

As the Woman's fingertips neared Medina's brow, a gleaming white marble hand reached from above and held her wrist tight. The statue of the soldier had come to life, and it stepped off its pedestal to defend Medina, its face turning toward the astonished advisor, and its mouth commanding him, in some strange, grating tongue which had never graced a human throat.

RUN, FATHER! RUN!

The Woman snarled and released her captive, raising her hand to touch the marble breastplate of the statue. The statue shattered into pieces, fragments burning with purple energy.

Medina ran as fast as he could, afraid to look back, but he could hear the Woman's strident cries, her angry voice, and the hoofbeats of her horse approaching. He could not outrun a horse, especially on an empty street...but he had no other ideas.

The Woman shouted in triumph; another few seconds and she would be close enough to grab him.

But then the street ahead turned into quicksand, too suddenly for her to avoid, cobblestones shifting beneath her horse to push it into the pit. As her horse went down, the Woman jumped from the saddle and tumbled onto the solid road ahead. She ran after Medina, leaving her horse to scream as it sank below the surface of the street, legs flailing, searching for solid ground to stand on.

The city itself seemed to come alive, and it was angry at her, fighting her at every turn. Bricks threw themselves from buildings and jumped from the street; fountains flung jets of water in her path, soaking her and causing her to lose her balance. As Medina dived around a corner a few dozen feet ahead of her, the Woman hesitated; there was a shadow growing around her. She looked up to see a stone, easily three hundred pounds, plummeting toward her.

She dived out of the way, and the stone missed her by bare inches. When she stood, Medina was gone.

The Woman screamed her frustration, and that scream echoed across the city, so that the people (who were still in the streets, marveling at the misfired trebuchet, the strangely cracked fountains, and the "earthquake" which had shaken so much masonry loose) could hear, and those that could see her stared at the source of that sound, wracked with hatred, pain, anger. Petty disagreements across the city expanded into brawls, and more than a few men and women slew each other over perceived slights that day.

She had lost him again. After over 700 years she had found him, tracked him...and now he was gone.

She smiled bitterly. She would find him again. It might take time, but Oreth would pay.

Oh, yes.

4 – KILLER IN THE CITY

The drifter awoke, lying on his back, with glaring lights and hazy figures in blues and whites moving above him, speaking in incoherent, unintelligible mumbles and murmurs.

"Where...where am I?" His eyes were weak and his vision bleary and unfocused, looking from right to left. "What's going on?"

A young man, dressed in a lab coat and wielding a light-emitting wand, stood above him, looking down into his face. *A doctor. I'm in a hospital.*

"Can you hear me?" The doctor's voice was echoing, hollow; it seemed to come after his lips had moved, reminding the drifter of badly-dubbed foreign films. The doctor raised his hands.

"How many fingers am I holding up?"

"....three."

"Good." The doctor's voice-track started syncing up with his lips. He took his light and examined the drifter's eyes as he spoke.

"You took a fall." He finished his examination and began jotting down notes on his clipboard. "Someone at the bus stop called us. It looks like you have a mild concussion, but I think you'll be fine." The doctor smiled, then turned to the side and pressed a button; moments later, a nurse was at the door. Her red hair contrasted sharply with the blue and white of her uniform, and she appraised the drifter before turning her gaze to the physician.

"Yes, doctor?"

"Make sure that this man rests for the next two or three hours." He finished his notes, clicked his pen shut, and tucked away his clipboard. "Check him again, and, if he's all right, he can go home."

The nurse nodded. "Yes, sir." The doctor stood, nodded to the drifter, and hurried out.

The red-headed woman walked to the curtains and pulled them, giving the drifter a nominal amount of privacy in the crowded hospital ward. Despite his injury, he couldn't help but notice that the nurse's outfit did not seem to fit her well; the hospital scrubs clung to her curves and her movements threatened to expose her midriff.

He laughed at his train of thought. *She probably just shrunk it in the wash or something.*

The nurse's hands moved, drawing the drifter's attention as she closed the curtains. *Those are rough hands. Those are working hands, hands that have been hurt and healed many times.*

"What exactly happened?" The drifter rubbed his head; his scalp was tender. "The doctor said that I fell?"

"Yes." Her voice was clear, like a bell ringing in the drifter's ears. *I knew that voice, once...where*

(a long time ago far far away when I was who I was)

was it?

A memory pierced the darkness, then; this woman, wiping her brow as she paused in her hammering, standing before an anvil made from a metal that had never, *could* never, exist. She was smiling at him, the reddish glow from the forge-fires matching her hair, and handing him a gladius which was still warm from the heat of its creation. Embedded in its surface were sapphires and rubies, and it glowed with a white-hot fire.

This will keep you safe.

Then it was gone.

She turned away from the curtains and her forest-green eyes blazed into his. "Unfortunately, we don't have time for that right now, Oreth. We have to go."

The drifter sat up, fighting against the wave of vertigo which swept over him. "How...who are you?"

The nurse's eyes widened. "You...you really don't remember?" The drifter shook his head. She took a deep breath, then seemed to refocus. "Well, it doesn't matter. I can explain everything to you, and I will, I promise, but right now we need to *go*."

"Stop it!" There were murmurs from the occupied beds surrounding him as his voice continued to rise. "How am I supposed to trust you when the last person I heard use that name, whoever's name that is, tried to kill me?" He paused, realizing what he had just said, then continued. "I'm tired of not knowing what's going on, of being afraid, of running away. I don't know *any* of you." He put his hand to his head, trying to shut out the feeling

(you do know them you did and you do)

and trying to stand up. "Who the hell *are* you people?"

The nurse stumbled back as the drifter spoke, as if his words were punches that he was throwing at her, injuring her with them. She took a deep breath. "I'm sorry, Oreth, I really am." The drifter's mouth dropped open; he hadn't expected an apology. "We need to go, *now*, or there might not be time to explain later." She turned her head to look past the curtain, then back. "Something's coming, right now, and it might kill you...might kill us both."

The drifter shook his head. "More bullshit." He folded his arms, his lip quivering as he held back tears. "Who...or what...is this 'something' and why does it want to kill me? Why should I believe you?"

The nurse stepped toward him, her face taut and her eyes moving quickly from one side to another. The muscles in her forearms bunched as she clenched her fists.

I think she's about to throw me over her shoulder like a sack of potatoes!

"We don't have *time*! Look, I'd love to explain it right now, Oreth, but we just..."

The sudden power outage cut her off, the hum of the backup generators kicking in underlying the sudden, confused babble which erupted in the room. The drifter staggered to the curtain, wrapping his fingers around the edge.

"Oreth, wait..."

He ignored her and pulled the curtain open on the room. In the semidarkness, he saw doctors and nurses and parents trying to calm patients and children. The emergency lights cast an orange hue over the nervous faces around him; in the next bed, a small boy was breathing in deep rattles as his mother struggled to get his aspirator in his mouth.

The elevator beeped.

A man, mature but vital, stepped out of the elevator. No eyes turned toward him, although his white suit and tie stood in sharp contrast to his ebony skin and hair. His dark eyes scanned the room until they alighted on the drifter.

The man in the white suit began walking toward the cordoned-off area where the drifter stood. He walked almost as if he were a soldier marching – slow, deliberate, and determined.

And, as he walked, the people around him died.

A young, pregnant teen went into premature labor and began screaming as she bled out from a catastrophic hemorrhage; her parents both suffered apocalyptic strokes at the same time. A doctor who was attempting to intubate a patient went into immediate cardiac arrest, falling down and clutching at his heart. Nicks and cuts on children and adults became infected; the necrosis racing toward the hearts of the victims like Olympians going for the gold, burning through veins and taking lives. No one within the white-suited man's reach survived; no one whom his hand could have touched lived to tell the story the next day. Screams echoed through the hospital room, and a mad rush for the door resulted in many more deaths, as wheelchairs were overturned and the young and old alike were trampled in the dash for safety.

The man in the white suit took no notice of any of this. He simply kept walking.

The time it took for him to cross the room was no more than twenty seconds, but the drifter's mind captured it all, captured the horror of it. He felt the power coming off of the terrible figure before him, and he was afraid.

This is Death. He could not move; his fate was inevitable. *This is truly Death itself. My God.*

A bright flash engulfed the room, blinding the drifter, and he heard a heavy *thud* in front of him. As his eyes recovered, he saw, interposed between himself and the man in the white suit, a figure coursing with electricity and other unnamable energies. The figure stood at least eight feet tall and was covered in gigantic metal plates, like a statue of a powerful warrior or a golem in a fantasy novel. Its hands clutched a huge, flaming hammer and every surface on its body was covered in runic script, conveying protection, strength, and courage.

The man in the white suit stopped and looked the figure up and down. His expression did not change, but the drifter could feel a sense of...curiosity? Amazement?

The giant sentinel turned its head to face the drifter and the visor opened to reveal the red hair and green eyes of the nurse.

"Run!" Her eyes were glistening like dew on leaves. "Run, now, Oreth! And take this." Her free hand came up and threw something small and metal toward the drifter, who caught it reflexively. It was a garden trowel, gleaming bronze.

"Remember me." He looked up and met her eyes, questioning, then nodded and closed his own.

The last the drifter saw of them was the monstrous construct leaping at the white-suited man, swinging its massive hammer at his immutable face.

5 – WATCHER ON THE BALCONY

Chicago. He reopened his eyes to a cityscape one hour earlier and over 700 miles away. He had arrived in an alley straight out of a gritty crime novel, complete with trash on the ground, neon lights advertising liquor and cigarettes, and a payphone on the corner.

Normally, one would feel safe from something if one were 700 miles away from it...but I don't. Not at all. I don't know if anywhere is safe from that...thing.

The drifter looked at his "parting gift." A trowel. A primitive building tool, with a blade made of pitted bronze lashed to a wooden handle. Why would she (*whoever she was)* give him something like this? Why was this important at all?

The drifter spun the tool around in his hand, grasping the handle, finding that it fit his hand well, like a glove that has molded to one's fingers. Idly, he knelt down and thrust the tip of the trowel into the dirt at his feet.

There was no sense of falling this time, no break in reality – he was simply somewhere else, *somewhen* else, a place and time when all tools were copper or bronze, when mankind had just learned to grow its own food and to predict the flood cycles of the rivers. He looked around and saw people, all of whom shared the drifter's skin, (*my people?*) in loose-woven clothes. They were leading animals and setting up a network of tents and other temporary dwellings. Children chattered, scurried, and laughed as their parents dug rows for seeds in the fine, fertile silt left by the rivers.

Tigris and Euphrates. Mesopotamia. The cradle of civilization.

Oreth (*for that* was *his name, wasn't it?*) stood, looking at this tribe with pride. He was not overly important or revered, but he was a builder, and what he would build would be the start of history – though none would remember his name, every future generation of mankind would live in his legacy, in what had been created by his hands, and of those who stood beside him, those who came after him. He would be immortal, in a sense, and that was not such a bad thing, was it?

No. Oreth's head snapped around; the voice was coming from the hole he had just begun. *Not such a bad thing, to live forever, Father. But not enough.*

Oreth stumbled backward, fell down. His head swiveled, searching for another source, something to explain the voice he heard, but he saw nothing. "Who are you?" No answer. "Are you a god? A spirit?"

No. Not a god. Not a spirit. I am an idea, the realization of a dream. You made me, Oreth. You and your people gave me strength, and now, here, we are joined for the first time to one another. This is a CITY, and that idea has made you into what you are now. Forev-

ermore we are one, and we shall be so forever...if you are willing.

"Willing?" Oreth stood and turned in a circle, running both hands across his cheeks. "You're offering me...what, exactly? Eternal life? That I will be...a city?"

Not a city, Oreth. <u>All</u> cities, this one and all of its children. As long as man lives together, builds homes and has neighbors, you will survive and guide them.

Oreth did not speak; his mouth had gone dry. He would live forever. He would become like a god, and see, learn, know, for all time.

Do you accept, Oreth?

The question was simple, and so was the answer.

Yes. He licked his lips, then spoke aloud. "Yes, I will."

For a moment, nothing happened, and Oreth had time to wonder if he had been tricked, deceived by some spiritual prankster.

Then it happened – his Second Birth, the gift of his Nature, his entrance into life as an Essential.

His perceptions expanded to encompass the whole of the encampment – he could *feel* each and every tent, footstep, and fire pit. He knew where each seed lay and where each animal rested.

There was more, however; each of these things knew *him*. He was connected to them, was one with them, and they recognized him as their master, lord, and father.

To say it was exhilarating would be an understatement fit for the most modest of maidens, akin to calling Leonardo da Vinci a tinkerer; Oreth's world was shattered and revealed for the flat, weak construct it was, a mere tablecloth, overlying the true reality: the reality of *ideas*, of ideas made flesh by joining men and women. He felt the snarl from the one who held the GREEN, all things that grow on the Earth, as he stepped into his power, and the clinical detachment of the master of REASONING at this new development. He was flush with strength and possibility, a man made into a god, and the world was his....in a sense.

"Oreth...are you all right? Is everything okay?" His wife approached him, a beautiful woman with dark hair and lightly-tanned skin. She placed a hand on his shoulder as she continued, "Is something wrong?"

Oreth turned, smiling, and kissed her deeply, marveling in the new sensations that even this simple act produced; when they broke away from one another, his wife's breathing was rapid and her eyes were wide.

"Oreth...what...what's going on?"

"Shhh..." Oreth spun her around, and held her close to him as they looked out over the new city. "Everything is wonderful, my dearest Eriana. Come with me; I have a fantastic idea for our house..."

~~~

Oreth's eyes opened once more to look upon the Chicago dirt at his feet. His vision was clouded by his tears, but, for the first time in a long time, they were not tears of sadness.

No more was he simply the drifter, a confused product of happenstance and chance, a beggar-bum who smelt of refuse and trash and wondered why the stoplights changed for him. No more.

All at once, it was like having those first moments back – remembering, finally, who he was and why he was. It was like standing on a balcony overlooking a great crowd. His vision
~~~

was cleared, and, although there was much in his memory that was still shrouded in the mists, <u>he</u> was no longer lost in them. He could see his beginning and where he was now, and if he could not see every step in between...well, it was infinitely better than it had been.

In his exultation, Oreth's mind instinctively began to reach out, to reconnect to the CITIES he had once been such an intimate part of (and they of him!), but he caught himself, held back, forcing the walls to stay up.

I could sense others. What if my amnesia, my loss of self, was the only thing keeping others from finding <u>me</u>? Maybe they don't know yet.

Maybe I can surprise them.

Maybe....I can save her.

Oreth was still not certain who "she" was, this red-haired woman who had sacrificed herself to save him from

(DEATH!)

something terrible...but he felt she was important. She might be a memory in the mists, forgotten for now...but she had fought for him, been willing to die for him, and he could not leave her like that. He had to save her. He looked at his hands, aware of the power within them now, cognizant of what he could do.

Each kindness repaid. I must help, if I can.

If she still lived. If he could find her.

I need help. But who? Who could he ask?

The payphone began to ring.

INTERLUDE

The hammer rose and fell, the sparks flying off the metal. Red hair dangled in her face, and she took a moment to wipe the sweat from her brow and tuck the lock behind her ear.

"This is good work, here."

The smith's hammer stilled and she turned her attention to the door of the shop. A large man, dark of skin and hair, stood in the entryway, wrapped in furs to keep out the chill of the northern winter.

"Thankee." The smith resumed her work.

"Don't see many women working metal." He ran a finger along the edge of a curved scythe hanging from the wall. "How'd you get into it?"

She didn't look up this time. "Was taught by my Da, before he fell. He was the best smith in the Isles."

"I knew him." His words brought her up short, her hammer stuttering in mid-air, and he laughed. "Best be careful, or your horse-shoe'll be ruint."

"You say you knew him?" The smith put her tools down and came around the counter to the newcomer. "How? When?"

"Calm down, lass. Calm down. Twas some time ago that I met him, when his talents at metalcraft had truly begun to be noticed." He held up a metal bowl. "We talked for a while, and I decided I would return someday to give him a gift." He set the bowl down and his head sagged.

"Shame I wasn't here soon enough."

The smith wiped her hands on a nearby cloth. "What gift d'ya have? Ma is still alive; she'd probably –"

The man shook his head, and a smile crept

across his face. "Don't worry." He pulled a knife off the wall, turned it this way and that. "Is this yours?"

She nodded, and he returned it to its perch. "I thought as much. Seems that your father passed on his talent for the Forge to you."

The smith blinked. "...What do you mean?"

~~~

Liara rose from her swoon, consciousness returning to her after a brief respite in Oblivion. She tried to sit up, but the bindings around her wrists and ankles were strong – she could see many of the same runes she used in her own crafting engraved on them. If she could have gathered her full power, she may have been able to break them, to unmake them...but that was impossible.

"Good morning." She turned her head to see the speaker – the man in the white suit, whom she knew as Azrael, whose Nature was Death. He was one of the oldest Essentials, if not *the* oldest, and his wide eyes were on her.

"I regret your reaction to my attempted contact with Oreth." His voice was smooth and cultured as he paced the room. Liara could feel
~~~

his presence draining the strength from her, the aura waxing and waning with his proximity.

"You wanted to kill him. I would die before I let you touch him."

Azrael stopped, eyes widening. "Kill him?" A thin chuckle escaped his lips. "If I wanted to kill him, he would already be dead." His voice took on a patronizing tone as he continued. "But we both know that, don't we?"

Azrael's power washed over her as he approached, the fatigue forcing her into silence. Azrael patted her face, and the contact seemed to sear her flesh.

Azrael took no notice of the tensing of her body as she bit back the scream. "We have unfinished business, he and I." He walked toward the window overlooking the hotel parking lot. The lights illuminated a couple screaming at each other, he with a beer in hand and she crossing her arms protectively over her pregnant belly; the man raised his hand and struck the woman to the ground.

Without warning, crimson red liquid started running, *gushing* from his eyes – he shrieked in horror...but then his shriek became a clotted gurgle as his tongue dissolved into bloody chunks in his mouth and ran between his teeth. His stomach ruptured and burst and his lungs filled with pus and blood.

His last moments were spent choking on his own fluids.

"You know." Azrael pulled the curtains shut. "I find it immensely considerate when someone volunteers their services as a test subject for new and interesting ways to die."

He turned away from the window, ignoring the terrified screams of the woman.

"Where do you think Oreth is?"

6 – VOICES FROM THE PAST

Oreth stepped cautiously to the phone. It appeared to be an ordinary Chicago payphone – tagged with red and green spray paint, scratched, dinged – but it was ringing, ringing as if its little life depended on someone answering.

Oreth brought his hand up to the phone, hesitated, and then brought the receiver to his ear.

"Hello?"

The phone crackled. "Oreth?" The voice on the other end of the line was fighting through the static. "Where are you?"

Oreth thought that today couldn't bring any more surprises. He was wrong.

"Who is this?" he asked.

"Edison. Look, where are you – this connection is crap; I can barely make you out. We need to talk."

"Why? What about?"

"I owe you one, man. You were there for me in Greece and I heard you were back, so...I wanted to repay you. Been a long time coming."

"Greece?" *When was I in Greece? Maybe....*

"Look, where are you? It's been too long and there's too much interference. I can't get a bead on you."

Oreth looked around. Did he dare trust this out-of-the-blue phone call? Was this a trap?

Or was it the only hope, the only lifeline he had?

I don't have a choice, do I? "Chicago."

"Oh! I was picking up signals from...never mind, I got you." The quality of the call went from barely-there to crystal clear. "Can you hear me now?"

"Yes, I can hear you. So how do you know me?"

"Hang on a second, Oreth; let me encrypt this line." Oreth heard a series of beeps and blips. "Alright – we met a long time ago, right around 490 BC if you can believe it." A moment of silence. "Aaaanyway..do you remember that story about the runner at Marathon?"

"No. I had amnesia."

"Oh! Yeah! Well, that was me. When I finished the run, my Nature came to me. You took me in and taught me the ropes...and now I'm in a position to return the favor."

Oreth tried hard to remember *anything* about this supposed meeting. He groped through the mists, recalling...a report?

"Magistrates, rejoice! The gods are with the sons of Athens; we have won!" The messenger, Pheidippides, was panting from his exertions as he stood before the leaders of the great metropolis of Athens. "Have joy!" He held his hands up in triumph...and then collapsed. An uproar arose from the collected senators and officials, and none noticed as one of their number, a man with darker skin than the olive tones of the others, scooped up the

unconscious form of the messenger. .

"Oreth? You there?" Oreth shook his head, trying to clear the fog.

Yes, I'm here. Then, realizing he hadn't spoken yet, he repeated the words aloud. "I think I remember you." He hesitated, licked his lips. "Did you...change your name?"

"Yeah! Good catch. After Edison sent that first phone message, I thought, 'Awesome!' and so I changed my name so that it would live forever. Guy's like, my hero." A moment's pause. "Too bad about that whole DC versus AC thing, though."

"All right, all right; what the hell is going on here, Edison?"

"Oh! Yeah, okay. Um...Azrael – that creepy dude in the white suit? – he took that woman...the nurse? He took her somewhere for something."

Oreth looked at the phone like it had just punched him in his face. He blinked a few times, then shouted into it.

"'Somewhere for something'?!"

A woman with two kids tapped on the glass of the phone booth. Oreth ignored her.

"Hey, relax, man, I know. Where she

is…isn't that important. If I know Azrael at all, he hasn't killed her. He's waiting for you."

"Why? What for?" Oreth closed his eyes, rubbing his temples. "I…I remember a woman…she's been hunting me for a long time…and she told me Azrael was looking for me."

"That's between you and him, man. All I know is what I saw on television: whatever happened, you've got a hell of an enemy after you."

"No, no…you know what, this phone is pissing me off. Hold on a second." Oreth closed his eyes and tried to focus, but the lady outside began yelling at him to hurry the hell up.

"In a minute!"

"Look, mister, I have two kids out here and it's cold and I need to call my husband so he can come pick us up because my car broke down…"

Oreth's eyes flew open and he leveled them on the woman. She recoiled from him like he had struck her. "I'll be done…in…a minute."

His eyes shut again, and

(*Gods it's been a long time since I've really had to work like this*)

he *flexed*, commanding the great network

that seemed to twine with his spirit, reaching out.

"I'll see you in a bit, Edison."

"Huh? Oh…okay. See you."

Click.

Oreth replaced the phone on its cradle and the impatient woman shoved past him on his way out, muttering something about the death of chivalry.

Oreth chuckled, and was about to say something witty

(I was at the death of chivalry, lady)

but then a Chicago city bus stopped in the street, pulled up to the curb. The folding doors opened as the bus screeched to a halt.

The grizzled bus driver looked over his tinted glasses. "Where to, mister?"

7 - ROB

"Just drive, Rob. I'll let you know when we get to my stop."

How did he...oh, my nametag, right.

"You got it, pal. Fare's $3.50, exact change."

The dark man in the ragged clothes chuckled and pointed at the fare machine, glowing with a green light.

"I've already paid."

Rob looked at the green light, stupefied for

a moment. "I...I guess so. Have a seat."

The drifter nodded and headed to a seat in the back of the old Chicago city bus. He looked like

(*a terrorist a terrorist on my bus*)

trouble, but Rob couldn't put his finger on why. He felt like he should be able to handle him if it came to it; his football days were behind him, sure, but at 42 he could still bench 350 pounds for 12 good reps, and this guy didn't look that strong, no way.

Rob glanced up at his newest passenger in the giant bus mirror as he stopped to drop off a group of coeds, giggling and laughing and smelling strongly of alcohol. Normally, Rob would be worried about the kids being out of control or getting in trouble, but his mind was on the man in the back.

The drifter was looking out the window, but... it looked to Rob like he was looking through the landscape instead of at it. His eyes were unfocused, lost in some other world, perhaps, or maybe just

(*Seeing things that we can't see*)

thinking.

Rob pulled up to another stop, let off an elderly couple. As they shuffled down the aisle and the stairs, Rob found himself hoping, almost praying

(*please God please don't leave me alone with him*)

that someone was waiting at this stop at 2:15 in the morning, but there was nobody there.

Rob started the bus moving again, his eyes avoiding the mirrors, allowing himself to imagine that the drifter was gone, that he had never gotten aboard...but he knew better. That feeling, that unease...the *wrongness*, was still there.

Rob checked his dashboard. 2:23. His gas light was on.

"Hey, mister." Rob turned on the signal. "Gotta stop at the 7-11 for gas; you want anything?"

Against his will, by reflex, his eyes flicked up to see his passenger.

The drifter's reflection was looking right at him, and in his eyes Rob could see

(*light shining like the heart of a star*)

something that he couldn't describe, like a doorway with a light on that you could see through the crack. For a moment, Rob was certain that those doors would swing open and the drifter's flesh would slough off, leaving only that inner force.

"There isn't time for you to stop, Rob." The drifter turned back toward the window, a small smile lifting the corners of his lips. "You have a pickup coming."

"Huh? I don't have a stop..." The bus ground to a halt of its own accord. Rob pushed on the gas pedal, but the engine did not respond.

"What the hell? Mister, I don't know what's goin' on, but I'm gettin' the fuck outta here!"

"Calm down, Rob." The drifter stood up and began walking toward him, taking slow, measured steps. "No one wants to hurt you, and I understand your confusion; believe me, I'm almost as confused as you are. Tell you what – do as I ask, and, if you want, I'll explain everything."

"Fuck no, mister, you'll explain it NOW!" Rob pushed away his fear, getting out of his chair and pulling himself up to his full, considerable height.

The drifter sighed. "Rob, you work for the

city of Chicago, don't you? Part of the civil service, public employee?

Rob curled up his brow. "Umm..yeah? So?"

"See, the thing is, Rob..." The drifter tilted his head as he looked at the near-panicked bus driver. "How to say this...I own you. Well, enough of you, anyway; the part of you that serves the City, that does your job. That's why you stopped to pick me up." The drifter stared him down as Rob laughed, a nervous titter that one would not expect to come from a man his size.

"Yeah, right, man. You need to get the hell off my bus."

The drifter's eyes were wide as he responded. "It's *my* bus, Rob, and you're *my* driver. Don't make me force you to do what I need you to do. I don't want to do that, but I will; there's too much going on right now that I don't understand, and there are things that must be done." The intense look the drifter was giving him faded, and he returned to his seat.

"Just sit down, Rob."

Rob froze. He was afraid, suddenly, but not because he thought this man was crazy, or that he was going to pull open his shirt and detonate the dynamite strapped to his chest.

He was afraid because he knew, somehow *knew*, that the drifter was telling the truth. There was something in the man's voice that compelled him, called to him, demanded his obedience.

"Well? Which is it going to be?"

Rob had been called many things in his four-and-change decades of life, but he had never been called a coward. He was afraid, yes, but there was something alluring about the light that Rob saw deep in the drifter's eyes.

The eternal struggle. No guts, no glory.

Before he could think better of it, Rob reached over and pulled the lever to admit his new passenger.

A dark-haired youth with olive skin, brightly-clashing clothes, and a beaming smile hopped on board. He popped out his headphones and laughed as he bounded up the stairs.

"Hey, man!" He put his hand out to Rob, who took it in a daze. The newcomer turned and laid his eyes on the drifter.

"Oreth!" He ran down the aisle, then made as if to embrace his traveling companion. Oreth put up a hand to stop him.

"Drive, Rob."

Rob nodded, but glanced out the door as he went to shut it – and his heart went cold. Above the roofs of the nearby buildings, he could see a great structure; a tall, metal monument that even a child should be able to recognize.

He was looking at the Eiffel Tower.

Somehow, he was in Paris.

8 - CHARMER IN THE BEDROOM

Oreth sat down with Edison as the bus began to motor away. Seeing this man stirred the same kind of mental vertigo he had felt when he had seen the nurse, that same sense that he had known the man once, perhaps a long time ago, perhaps only in a dream.

"What's going on?" He leaned forward, holding the younger man's dark eyes with his own. "Tell me everything you know, Edison, and no bullshit; I'm tired of half-answers and cryptic riddles. Tell me the truth."

Edison rubbed the back of his neck, a nervous smile playing on his lips. "Everything, huh? You sure about that?" The look in Oreth's eyes made him laugh, and he waved his hands. "Just kidding, man, just kidding, but...this could take a while."

"If I remember anything about anything, then no one should be able to find us while we're on this bus. I have it moving between cities, flipping back and forth while he drives." He nodded his head toward Rob. "We've got time."

Edison nodded. "Nice trick." A smile. "Should do for now, I suppose; after all, you have been gone for almost two thousand years without getting got, huh?"

Oreth tapped his fingertips together. "Tell it, Edison. What is going on?"

As Oreth spoke those words, they seemed to echo in his mind. All at once, he was standing in a classical Greek building, with a young man, head in his hands, crying and laughing all at once. The young man looked up at Oreth with big eyes.

"What is going on?" the young man who would, centuries later, be sitting in a city bus

driven by a former college football player, had asked. "What happened to me, Senator? It's like I can hear everything, see everything...It almost hurts, but I don't want it to stop." His eyes had pleaded, begged. "Is something wrong with me?"

Oreth had shaken his head. "Not any more, Pheidippides. Your mortal frailties are gone; you have been gifted with your Second Birth. You have left mortality behind, and become unto a God." Oreth had put a hand on his shoulder. "You need to be careful, now, or you may accidentally do grave harm to your Nature...or yourself. Be cautious, be wise, and remember always that your first responsibility is to your Nature, not to yourself."

The young man had nodded, and the nod of the Hellenic times translated into the nod of the 21st Century.

"Well, here's what I know: I had my Second Birth and you were there to teach me the basics of who we are, what we could do. You were...abrupt, I guess is the best word for it; you told me what you thought I needed to know, then sent me off to do it." Edison laughed. "It was a hell of a lot more education than most of us get, sure, but whenever I had a question about anything I felt like I was pissing in your cereal. Made me wonder why you bothered at all."

Oreth rubbed his temples, but the memories did not come. *I wonder myself.* He refocused on his companion "What about the...woman? The dark-eyed woman? The one who is looking for me?"

Edison shook his head. "You never mentioned her back then." He grinned and leaned back in his seat, then dropped Oreth a wink. "Of course, back then you had an awful lot of women; it would have been easy for any of them to feel jilted, get superpowers, and come after you all pissed off, I guess."

Oreth blinked. "...Lots of women?"

Edison's smile grew. "Yep. You were lord of your domain, a Senator of Athens, you ruled city-states...you had an entourage around you pretty consistently, but..." Edison hesitated, then shook his head. "Never mind, it's not important."

"Yes, it is; Edison, I barely remember *anything*. If I'm going to figure this thing out, figure out what is going on, you need to be up front with me. *What* isn't important?"

Edison licked his lips. "Normally, I don't like to say bad things about people, but...you were kind of an ass-hat to them, man. They fawned all over you and you just...ignored them, shoved them out of your way if you were in a mood. I once walked in on you with one of them, you know, *in flagrante delicto*, and you just walked away to talk, leaving her on the bed." He chuckled, shaking his head.

Oreth's brow knitted together. *Was I...*He dug into the maze of his mind, trying to re-member, trying to pierce that veil, the thinned fog. There were a few images, a few sensa-tions...but nothing clear, nothing to explain to him where that disdain for other humans had come from.

"All right." He stopped his mental search, waving his hand and giving Edison his atten-tion. "Granted that I was apparently an ass-hat; how does that lead in to the current situation?"

"I watched the whole thing on CC camera when Azrael came to get you. I don't know ex-actly who the babe was, but she had obviously gotten wind that he was coming and found you first. So..." Edison was cut off as the bus came to an abrupt stop.

Oreth called up front, "What's the hold-up, Rob?"

The reply: "Roadblock. City cops checking folks out to see if they're drunk." He laughed, fear underlined with excitement evident in the sound. "Kinda wish I was, you know."

The corners of Oreth's mouth twitched, and he sent out the smallest extension of his will. The city cops, in unison, snapped to attention and waved the bus through. Rob raised his hand to one of the cops as they passed.

"Umm...that was weird." Rob glanced in the mirror and his mouth moved as if to ask the question...but then he didn't.

Oreth gestured for Edison to continue.

"Right! So, whoever she was, this nurse went to bat for you. Azrael took her out, obviously; it's a foregone conclusion." Edison's smile was bitter this time; his eyes flinched, an almost invisible motion, but Oreth caught it.

"So we have no idea what this...Azrael...wants with the girl?" Oreth noticed that he was holding his breath, and let it out in a rush.

"Well, not really." Edison shrugged. "I'm

sure that he wants to use her as leverage, get you to do something for him, though what *you* could do for *him* I'm not quite clear on. See, the thing about Azrael," he went on, a devious grin splitting his face, "is that he's not evil."

Oreth blinked. "He's not? Cause it sure seemed to me like he was, what with the murder of innocent people in the hospital and everything."

"Nope. He's not. It's just everything that he *does* is evil."

"Say again?"

"No, see, just look. People don't like dying, don't like those close to them dying, but *everyone* dies when Azrael goes by. It's just what he is, what he does." Edison spread his hands. "Most people call the random deaths of innocent civilians 'evil,' but I think that Azrael is kinda past that."

Oreth opened his mouth to reply, then shook his head. "We shouldn't be worried about character motivations here, I guess," he said. "What are we going to do when we get there? I'm not keen on going up against, well, *Death*, especially out of practice like I am."

Edison looked out the window, where the

scenery had changed from Paris streets to New York thoroughfares, to Mexico City boulevards and Los Angeles broadways, before answering.

"You can't fight Azrael." His voice was soft, as were his eyes. "Azrael is Death, the finality, the end of everything. Nothing survives if he decides it should not – not even us. We can't beat him in a head-on fight, no way." He stretched his lips, attempting a smile. "But, hey, 'the bigger they are, the harder they fall' right?" Edison paused, considered, laughed. "Pun not intended. Anyway, if you can't win in a straight-up fight, you don't fight straight-up."

"What do you mean?"

"Well, look at the legends, right? No one fights Death and wins. Nobody. You've got to trick Death, hide from him, escape and come back." Edison shrugged. "I dunno. Worth a shot, right?"

Oreth stared at his companion, mouth hanging open, then laughed. "You mean we should go in there and just *wing* it?"

Edison smiled a real smile this time. "Don't they say you should do something that scares the hell out of you at least once a day?"

"Hmph. This is hardly the first thing that

has scared me today." The corners of Oreth's mouth turned down.

Edison's smile disappeared. "Let's hope it won't be your last, then."

"How do we find them?"

Edison waved his hand, pulled out his cellphone. "No sweat. As they said in that Percy Jackson movie...and the book was *way* better, you know?... 'GPS from the gods, coming right up.'"

A few taps on the screen of the ordinary, if expensive, phone brought up a three-dimensional map of the Earth with several thousand glowing flags dotting its surface.

"So here we are." A moving pair of flags turned from red to blue. "Now, normally, Azrael can't be found on here, but if we're lucky..."

"Wait." Oreth glanced up at Edison. "Why can't he be found?"

"Oh, right. Well, Azrael's been around a long, *long* time, you see, and he knows things...spells, chants, ways to make reality do things that his Nature doesn't account for. Kind of like cheat codes for the universe."

"Like the *athalaxa*." Oreth's mind reached back, remembering the poor businessman in

Japan.

Edison's jaw dropped. "You...you remember the *athalaxa?* You told me never to use it, that it was just far too cruel a fate to be visited upon anyone."

Oreth stared off for a moment, lost in the fogs of memory again. "I...I saw her, that woman, do it to someone..." He turned to Edison, confusion reigning in his eyes. "I took it off him, Edison. I didn't even know how I knew to do that, then, but something in me did. I..." He waved it off. "Not that important. So, Azrael can't be seen normally. He has some sort of spell to keep him cloaked. Is that about right?"

"Got it in one, my man. And, unfortunately, I don't know the name of the girl, so finding her would take longer. I can do it if I have to, but..." Another flag turned blue, one of a pair, on the east coast of the United States. New York, New York.

"Jackpot! Figures, too, that he wouldn't even have taken her out of the city. Zoom." The miracle-phone complied, grainy three-dimensional images transforming into a beautifully-rendered parking lot.

Of a Motel 6.

"Seriously?" Oreth searched Edison's face for any sign he was joking. He found none. "A Motel-6? Death is hanging out at a Motel 6?"

Edison shrugged. "Maybe he was attracted by the free cable." He smiled, but his voice gave the lie to his humor. "Can you get us there?"

Oreth did not reply; instead, he called up to Rob. "Next left, Rob, and stay in the right lane; we're going to hit a parking lot kind of suddenly, so don't go too fast, all right?"

"Umm...yeah, no problem. You got it." Rob's voice still quavered as he fought to keep the confusion, bordering on panic, from showing. He followed directions, turning left, merging into the right lane...

And then he was in the bright lights of a parking lot, dodging a pedestrian, a woman who would later swear that that bus "came out of nowhere."

"Shit!" He slammed on the brakes and spun his wheel, balancing the bus on two wheels for just a second before it stopped, no one hurt, in front of the Motel 6 office. Profanity spewed from his mouth like Old Faithful.

"Good stop, Rob." Edison was laughing at the bus driver's stream of expletives. Oreth shook his head, and Edison's chuckles subsided, but he kept smiling.

The bus door opened into the fluorescent darkness of the Motel 6 parking lot. Edison dashed down the stairs, giving the bus driver a thump on the shoulder as he left.

Oreth stopped on his way out and turned to Rob.

"Go home." He gestured to the highway behind the lot. "This isn't something you need to be part of. Go. Try to forget what you saw; it'll be easier for you."

Rob shook his head. "Mister, I ain't ever run from anything in my life." He laughed, and this time it was real laughter, full of *joie de vivre*. "I don't know what the hell is going on, but I'm forty-two years old, I got no family of my own, and you've just totally *fucked* my world." He smiled, almost a grimace. "Way I see it, I've got two choices; either I can hate you, try to stab you in the back, or I can try to find my own way to handle it."

Rob inhaled through his nose. "I guess I'm not sure which way to go yet."

Oreth put his hand out for Rob to take. "Let me know when you figure it out."

~~~

The Motel 6 loomed above the two Essentials like the bleak edifice of a concentration camp's gas chamber. The neon lights flickered, creating movements seen only in the periphery, shadows that were impossible to pin down, to determine what, if anything, was *really* moving. The bloodstain on the asphalt seemed, to Oreth's eyes, to be an echo of some past horror – he could swear that there was a hollow scream tethered to the smear.

"Well." Edison's voice was cheerful, but his eyes were wide, flickering like candle flames in the dark. "Into the lion's den, right?" He swallowed. "Ready?"

Oreth squared his shoulders. "Pick a cliché, Edison. Belly of the beast, lion's den, whatever; let's go. Which room do you think he's in?"

Edison scanned over the motel for a moment, then pointed up to a room on the second floor.

"The potted plants."

Oreth looked up and saw that, while in front of the other rooms the shrubs just needed
~~~

a bit of water, the decorative greenery in front of one particular doorway had withered like it was the middle of a Siberian winter.

The two of them climbed the stairs to the room. Number 224. The blinds were shut, but a light was on inside. The door was slightly ajar. The two men shared a glance, then Oreth twisted the handle and opened the door.

The light from the parking lot cast Oreth's shadow across the small, seedy hotel room. The TV flickered, sending ghost lights scampering up the walls. The dingy beige carpets were broken by a thin, flimsy bed which held a single occupant – a red-haired woman with tatters of hospital scrubs her modesty's only defense. She was semiconscious, chained to the bed with shackles of some

(*armetium*)

eldritch metal, glowing with crimson and emerald runes. Oreth ran to her side and Edison followed after.

"Forgive...no...stop." The woman was murmuring in a dream-haze, head lolling on the mattress from side to side.

"Do you know what these are?" Oreth ran his hands across the chains.

Edison looked at the bindings. "No, but this is no ordinary metal. I would guess that the Forge made this, but no telling." He shook his head. "But if the Forge *were* here, I bet he could get her out of this."

Oreth gazed at her face, and a half-formed memory

(A whisper in the ear. "Everything made can be unmade, Oreth.")

of a lesson learned early in his existence tugged at him. He traced his fingers over the runes, singing to them.

<<Open.>>

A surge welled up in Oreth's head – there was a sudden heat behind his eyes – then a soft *click* as the locks disengaged.

"Holy shit! How did you do that?" Edison reached forward to grasp the manacles. "Awesome! Now we just need...to..." His voice trailed off, and Oreth turned to see what had come to Edison's attention, a wave of fatigue washing over him.

In the bathroom doorway stood the white-suited figure of Azrael, whose eyes glimmered with pleasure.

"Oreth." He extended his arms as if to embrace his visitor. "It is good to see you again. We have important business to discuss, you and I."

Oreth tried to keep his knees from shaking, though whether it was the fear or the weakness he felt in them, he did not know.

Oreth nodded toward the woman and Edison. "Let them go, and I'll stay and talk, if that's what you want."

Azrael tilted his head, keeping his expression of casual interest, then nodded. "Very well." He raised a finger. "But if you are thinking of trying to...leave, I have something I should show you."

Azrael opened his right hand to reveal a luminous visage, a face moving in and out of green-white mists, constantly shifting but easily recognizable as the nurse. After a moment, he closed his hand, and it was gone as if it had never been.

"I have your friend's life, her essence, in my power. Leave and...unpleasant things could happen."

Oreth did his best to look indignant. "I said I would stay and talk, and that's what I'm going to do. What about your end?"

Azrael nodded, smiling with the corners of his mouth, and beckoned for Edison to come forward. Trembling with terror, Edison shuffled to the bed and picked up the woman's limp form. He began to back away, and as he passed Oreth, he tugged on Oreth's sleeve. Oreth spared him a quick glance.

Edison's lips moved. "Be smarter." Then he was gone, out the door.

Oreth turned back to face Azrael. He had been in the presence of other Essentials before, he knew, and each one had some sort of "feeling," some sort of effect on their environment, a reflection of the Nature held within. What he felt now, however, was more than that. Other than himself and Azrael, there was *nothing* alive in this room.

There were no mice hiding in the walls, no cockroaches on the floor. The houseplants had withered and died; even the air and water were sterile, with no bacteria or spores within them. This room was occupied by Death, and Death spared nothing within.

Azrael gave his trademark corner-smile and motioned for Oreth to sit in one of the complimentary hotel chairs.

"No, thank you. I'll stand if it's all the same." Oreth crossed his arms over his chest.

Azrael chuckled, a rich warm sound which took Oreth off guard. As he spoke, his face was lively, animated. "Did you know that you are the first of our kind I have spoken to like this in almost two thousand years? Face to face, without groveling, without mindless blubbering?" He paused for a moment as Oreth processed this information before continuing. "That's right. I have not had a decent conversation since, oh, the fall of Rome, actually."

The Fall of Rome. The dream. Why? The words sent a shiver up Oreth's spine as he sought to respond.

"Should I feel sorry for you? You murder indiscriminately; people die for the crime of getting within arm's reach of you. Is it any wonder that you don't have anyone to talk to? Stop wasting our time with this 'poor me' bullshit. " Oreth's eyes were hard as he glared at his companion. "Get to the point, Azrael."

Azrael's eyes widened, pupils dilated, and his voice leveled off – the near monotone of controlled anger.

"Do not so speak to me, Essential. I have

lived longer than any others of our kind, and I will outlive all of you. Show respect or be taught respect."

"Am I supposed to be impressed?" Oreth threw his hands into the air. "Show me how powerful you are, then! Strike me dead! I've spent God knows how long afraid of things I couldn't remember!" Oreth leveled a finger at Azrael's face.

"You honestly think you scare me? Well, you're right; you do. To death, literally. I'm terrified." His voice turned serious.

"But I think you're bluffing."

Azrael was staring in open disbelief. "What happened to you in your exile? You've..."

"Changed, yeah. So I've heard. Maybe it's just that I've spent the last six months, and however long before that, being *human*." Oreth spread his arms. "Humans don't fear the dark anymore, Azrael. Do you know why? It's not because there aren't scary things in it." A thin, reedy chuckle. "After all, people like you and me are in it. No, it's because, if you're afraid of everything you *can't* do anything about, then you'll never fix the things you *can* do something about."

Azrael looked away, down at the floor. "Do you remember Eriana?"

Oreth was confused by this sudden change of subject. "What?"

Azrael's eyes came back up. "Eriana. Your wife, at one time."

"...of course I remember her. Why?"

"What do you last remember about her?"

Oreth opened his mouth to say *I remember the day I became an Essential,* but then another memory pierced his skull with dull fire, tinged with shame.

"I...I left her." His gaze fell, looking without seeing as the past rolled over him. "The city we had built had grown, become self-sufficient...become legendary, even. I said..." Oreth's hand went to his forehead, grasping, trying to hold on to the memory before it fled. "I said that she was...was holding me back, that a god could not be constrained by mortal ties." Tears welled up in Oreth's eyes as he remembered his own reflected image in Eriana's, the weeping as he turned and willed himself halfway across the world.

Azrael nodded and began examining his fingernails as he spoke. "She hates me, you know."   Oreth's head came back up and his eyes narrowed.

"She became Vengeance, and Death is both friend and enemy to her, the instrument of Vengeance and the harbinger of its arrival." Azrael's voice was jovial, but his eyes were sad. "But there *is* one person she hates more."

"...Who?" asked Oreth, afraid he already knew the answer.

Azrael tilted his head. "You, of course, old friend." He took a step forward.

Oreth felt the aura around his adversary strengthen, and weariness washed over him like the sea at high tide. He struggled to stay standing.

"You see, you left her to...well, to serve yourself, I suppose. Not uncommon for a newborn Essential, really, to get lost in the Nature, exploring, facilitating." He stepped again. "Unfortunately, you abandoned her, left her in a place terrified of you, and they vented their fears upon your wife. You had reigned as God-King in that place so long, with her at your side, and then, when you left her? It didn't take long for those who had feared you to take advantage of your absence." *Step.* "They left her there, left her dying, until her Nature came for her. None of them survived."

Step. Darkness was hovering at the edge of Oreth's vision.

"I promised her she could have you." Azrael's voice drilled into Oreth's fading consciousness. "She wants to kill you, of course, but I won't let her." *Step.* "At least, not if you give me what I need from you."

"W...wh...what do you want?" Oreth went down on one knee, trying to hold his head up. He tried to focus, to disappear, but he could not muster the will.

Azrael stopped in front of him and knelt down, something which could have been concern in his face as he stared into Oreth's eyes.

"You're going to keep a promise, Oreth. You're going to set me free."

Oreth lost his last grip on the waking world, and fell into nothing.

9 - TALE OF TWO CITIES

Liara woke to the whap-whap of flesh smacking flesh. It took her a moment to realize that someone was slapping her face.

Her eyes opened and refocused in the bright lights of a city bus.

How did I get here? Her attempt at vocalization resulted in a small groan escaping her lips.

"Hey, you're awake!" came a loud, vibrant voice. She looked toward her feet and saw a young Greek man in neon clothes smiling at her. *An Essential,* she realized. *He feels...connected, a part of everything.*

"I'm Edison." He mimed tipping an imaginary hat. "You are...?"

"What?" Liara's mind was still cloudy, her consciousness struggling to focus.

"Your name. Title. *Issm. Nombre.* Appellation." He waved his hands in the air. "You know, the thing people call you."

"Oh...Liara. I'm Liara."

"Nice to meet you, Liara. Oreth and I came to bust you out of there, but..."

"Oreth?" Liara's eyes widened and she sat up. "Where is he? Is he all right?"

"Umm..." Edison hesitated, eyes moving back and forth as he licked his lips.

"What happened?" Her voice broke on the last word, and her hands shot out and gripped Edison's shirt, pulling him close. "What *happened?*" she repeated. "Is he dead?"

"Hey, lady, relax!" Edison tugged at her strong hands, but her grip did not falter. "I don't think he's dead, but...well, Azrael seemed like he *really* wanted to talk to him, and he said that if Oreth tried to leave, he would kill you."

"What?" Liara's fingers loosened and her eyes narrowed. "That's not..."

"Umm, sorry." Edison's grin broke through. "As fantastic as this is for me, really, we might want to hold this conversation after you put on something less...revealing?" He gestured at her outfit.

Liara looked down at her body. The clothes she had been wearing, her nurse's uniform, was torn and scorched in several places from the battle at the hospital; normal fabric just couldn't take the heat of the Forge's power. He was right; it wasn't covering much anymore. She flushed, then forced herself to meet his eyes.

"Give me some privacy, then, if you don't mind!" She stood, refusing to give away her embarrassment. Still grinning, Edison turned around.

Liara undressed; her focus still a bit fuzzy from her near-Death experience, so it took her longer than usual to picture what she wanted; underwear, grey pants, white blouse, forged from metal but soft and supple, the product of the Forge, the Metalcrafter, worker of wonders.

She turned to see Edison's eyes in the bus's rear view mirror. Her face steamed, blood carrying shame and anger in equal quantities

"Ready, then?" He turned, smiling...until Liara's fist slammed into his face, crashing him into the front of the bus.

"Holy shit!" Rob jerked the steering wheel in surprise. "Knock it the fuck off!"

Edison rose from the impact site, lip bleeding and energy crackling around him like a charged generator. His casual demeanor had vanished in an instant, leaving an angry god – a god who spoke to everything that thought, a god connected here and there and everywhere.

"Look, all due respect, and I don't know about you two, but we go over and *I'm* done. I'd rather not be done just yet, if you don't mind."

The two stared at each other for a few interminable seconds, the air still between them.

Liara broke the silence. "Oreth?"

A moment passed before Edison nodded. "Oreth." The charge in the air began to dissipate, though the smile did not immediately return to his face.

"What's the plan?" Liara sat in one of the

seats, facing the aisle. "If Azrael has him..."

"Yeah, it's bad." Edison took up a position nearby, standing with his arms crossed and leaning against a window. "I wasn't surprised that Azrael took him, honestly, but..."

"Wait, wait." Liara raised a hand to stop him. "You *knew* Azrael was going to take him?" Her fists clenched and her jawline tightened. "You let him walk in there to get..."

"Yeah, I did. He wanted to save *you*, crazy lady. It was either I go with him or he goes in himself." Edison shrugged. "Normally, some-one walks right into Azrael's arms I'm just gonna say 'Well, good luck to you,' but...well, I don't know. He wanted to save you, and I wasn't going to let him go in alone. Not that he would have cared, before."

Liara's eyes went distant. *Before.* So long ago, when the world was smaller and things

(his smile his laugh)

made sense. The word tasted like antique furniture, rich and mysterious as she rolled it off her tongue. "Before..."

"Yeah – he was different then." Edison sat. "The centuries have changed him a lot, you know."

Liara shook her head. "I didn't have time to get to know him again; Azrael came before I could get him out of that hospital." She leaned closer. "How has he changed...Edison? Is that it?"

Edison's smile broke out of hiding. "Yeah, that's it. Well, let me see..."

"Hey!" interrupted Rob from the front. "You two mind if I put on some music? Listening to you talk is just...weird."

Edison laughed. *I like this guy.* "Sure, man. Just not any of that easy-listening crap, all right?"

Rob saluted in the mirror. "No sir. I only roll with sweet rock, my friend."

Edison gave him a thumbs-up, then his face returned to a more serious mien.

"Well, I remember something that he told me once – he said, 'Don't throw your life away. You have the potential to live forever, to serve as eternal testament to your Nature, to its accomplishments and its impact on humanity. Nothing is worth dying for, except the preservation of the Nature itself.'"

She nodded. "Self-preservation was always very important to him. It was hard to

(love)

connect with him. He was always holding back."

Edison chuckled, color flooding his face. "He talked to me about that once, when I was new to the game." His eyes looked upward, remembering. "He was always telling me that I shouldn't pry too deeply into the secrets of others, 'lest yours get stolen while you are away.'" Another chuckle. "He was a paranoid S.O.B. back then. Now...you didn't see his face, Liara. He didn't even remember me, remember you, remember Azrael. None of it!"

Liara's eyes gleamed as Edison continued. "He didn't remember anything except sorta what he was, and he was willing to go in, balls to the wall, and take on Death."

Edison leaned in close. "Tell me the truth." His eyes held hers. "If this had been two thousand years ago, would he have stood up to Azrael for you? Even when he knew you?"

Oh, she wanted to lie, wanted to say the words that would make the man she loved seem to have returned that love...but no. She shook her head. An image played in her mind, of the nobility in his face, the determination...and the absolute indifference to everything except the welfare of his Nature. No, he would not have done that.

"No." Her voice was a whisper, full of pain. "In his early days, perhaps...but even then, he was so concerned about being immortal – about *lasting*, is how he put it, that his purpose was to *last* – that he wasn't willing to do much of anything that could have jeopardized his existence." She hesitated a moment. "He...he really went in after Azrael? To save me? He wasn't afraid?"

Edison started to chuckle...but the chuckle turned into a deep, belly laugh, ending with him rolling on the floor and tears leaking out of his eyes, the laugh becoming soundless echoes - a pantomime of laughter.

"What's so damn funny, Edison?" Liara's fists had bunched up again – his insane laughter had made her start worrying that he was losing it, and that was not something she could afford right now.

"I...I'm..oh, God, are you crazy?" His words came out in stutters, interrupted by laughter, and wiped his eyes and cheeks and sat back upright. "Not afraid? He was terrified! He had no fucking clue who this guy was – just that when he walks around, people die, and that he had you trapped, maybe, and all he knew about you is that you used to know him...apparently. He just sucked it up and drove on, as they say in various ways in every military on the planet." Edison stood and started pantomiming to go along with his narration.

"So then! He kicks open the door and heads in there! We see you, he opens the locks - just as easy as you please, thank you very much – and then Azrael shows up. Death-God over here says that we – you and me – could leave as long as Oreth stayed to talk. And he did! No hesitation, just a 'let's do the right thing let my pals go you crazy death-machine.'"

Edison sat back, beaming a huge smile at Liara's astonished face. "Doesn't that just beat all?"

Liara was stunned. *Nobody* walked up to Azrael and told him...well, anything. Azrael was the 'bogeyman,' because Death followed in his footsteps, danced in his breath, reveled in his caress. Even the Essentials, immortal beings, were subject to Azrael's displeasure. There had been a few times when, fresh from their Second

Breath, someone with a Nature like Hope or Peace decided to interfere in Azrael's affairs. Afterward, there would be a *new* Essential carrying that Nature, who would be taught better, by anyone who cared to intervene.

Oreth had been terrified of Azrael. They had met only a few times, as far as Liara knew, and it was never because Oreth sought Azrael out. Indeed, Oreth went out of his way to avoid places where Azrael was even suspected of being; still, every few centuries, Azrael would appear, and his arrival would be preceded by plague, war, famine, and devastation.

And was that so wrong? Was it so wrong to be afraid of something that could end your existence; to fear something that could, on a whim, destroy you? Still, the idea of Oreth standing up to Azrael seemed...well, it was a wonderful fantasy, and if he *had* done it...

"What are we going to do, Edison?" Her words startled her out of her own reverie. "He risked himself for us. We can't just let him die...or whatever it is that Azrael has planned for him!"

Edison gaped at her, then shook his head. "Umm...believe it or not, I wasn't planning to."

He rubbed his chin. "Do you have a plan? I sure don't, not yet."

"I don't know!" She threw her hands in the air. "We can't just charge in there and save him – Azrael would have our hearts for dinner."

"Possibly with fava beans." Edison's eyes dipped in thought, then brightened. "Well...what if we challenged him to some sort of game? A contest? A challenge? You know, like the stories and the movies and stuff?" He leaned forward. "Maybe we could win Oreth back from him!"

"A...game. Are you serious?" Liara rubbed her hand across her eyes. "You want to play a *game,* with someone who makes you feel like...well, your age, I suppose...every time you get close to him? And what shall it be?" she continued, her voice rising in pitch. "Chess? Parcheesi? Spades? Oh, I know, Twister! Bet he'd love that!" Her eyes burned into Edison's face, and he shrank from the intensity of it. "If you can't come up with something better than that, I'm throwing you off this bus and leading a fucking cavalry charge myself!"

Edison leaned forward, controlled fury etching his face. "No...shit. I think this is our best bet, Liara. All the old legends..."

"Are legends!" Liara was red, and violence was etched onto her every word and action. "That's all they are!" She stood and looked down at her companion. "You'd think that, having lived as long as you have, you'd know that, Edison."

Edison's face had fallen and his eyes had reddened. Tears glistened at their corners, and Liara realized that, silly and useless as his ideas might have been, he was *trying,* he was *thinking,* and he *cared.* She, on the other hand, was tearing him apart without offering a single idea in return.

It made her feel like a real bitch.

"Hey." She sat next to Edison, reaching out for his hand. "I'm sorry. I'm just worried about him. I wouldn't have let him die before, if I could help it...and I'm not about to now, you know?"

Edison nodded, his throat working. "Me neither." His words were thick with emotion. "I got to know the 'new' Oreth a bit and...I like him. I think he'd go to bat for me...and I'm not going to let him down."

"Fair enough, but I don't think a game is

the way to go. Maybe as a last resort, but there has to be something else we can do."

Edison scratched his head. "Well, unless we can find something to trade him for Oreth, something that he really, *really* wants..."

Liara's head came up. Edison noticed and leaned toward her.

"What is it?"

"I think I know what we can trade."

"What? What?"

"The Alabaster Egg."

10 – INTO THE MISTS

Edison looked at Liara for a few seconds. "Al...what's an alabaster egg got to do with anything?"

Liara shook her head. "Not *an* alabaster egg. *The* Alabaster Egg."

Edison rolled his eyes. "Ookay...so what's *the* Alabaster Egg?" he asked, making air quotes as he did so.

"Well it might not exist – in fact, it probably doesn't – but when I was younger, I did a lot of traveling."

Edison nodded. "I think that a lot of us do that, at first."

"Exactly. Because of my Nature I was interested in the various ways that people thought we all came about. It was really fascinating to hear, because there are a lot of myths about the creation of the world – the Biblical Genesis story, the Olympian gods and Titans. When I found other Essentials, though, some of them would tell old stories, stories about how, when the Universe was new, all of the leftover creative 'juice' was stored in an egg-shaped vessel. Most of them claimed that the vessel was made of purest alabaster."

Edison spread his hands and started ticking off his fingers. "Okay. Let's assume for a second that this Egg actually exists. I'll ignore the fact that it's just a 'story or legend.' Why hasn't Azrael gone to find it, if he wants it? Second, why would the 'Powers that Be' leave something like that lying around? Third, how the hell are *we* supposed to find it?"

Liara paused a moment, thinking, trying to

remember – legends, myths from a society peopled by souls who might not see one another for decades or centuries on end.

"Well, in the stories, they used to say that something like the Egg couldn't help but make an explosion of life and genitive energy wherever it rested – kind of like the opposite of Azrael, you know?"

Edison leaned back in his bus seat as Rob took a hard right onto the Interstate. "So, how many acres is the rainforest? Actually, *which* rainforest?"

"We're not going to hunt through the entirety of the rainforest, dumbass." Edison snickered at Liara's insult. "We need to get help...unless the satellites can tell you where it is?" Her look turned speculative.

Edison pulled out his cellphone, punched a few keys and swiped a couple of times. Light started flashing across his open eyes, light shed by satellite images he was viewing at speeds which any mortal observer would believe impossible.

After five or six minutes of this, the lights stopped flashing and Edison blinked.

He didn't blink that whole time. Edison

smiled and shook his head.

"No luck, darlin'." He gave her a wink and a smile.

Liara shook her head. "I didn't think so." Her head moved, turning to look out of the window again.

"Hold on." Edison cocked his head to the right, like he was listening to something. Another few minutes passed with Edison nodding, listening, nodding again as Liara tapped her foot.

Edison's posture and attitude returned to normal; Liara pounced. "So? What was that?"

Edison's eyes were still a bit hazy as he replied, "We need to go speak to someone. She should be able to help us." He shrugged.

Liara wanted to ask, of course, but she held her tongue – something in Edison's gaze, like he was...someplace else.

Edison's eyes cleared. "An old...friend...of mine might be able to find it. She commands the Way, all paths, the roads to all goals. And she wants to see us; at least, that's what she just told me."

Liara could no longer hold it in. "Who?"

Edison smiled, but his smile was that of

someone who had just bitten into something unpleasant, but dared not offend his host.

"Despoina, the Lady of the Labyrinth. In Crete." He shrugged, but the tension never left his face. "I don't know how she knows about it or what, but I suppose I shouldn't be that surprised."

"Is something wrong with her? Why do you look so nervous? Is she dangerous?"

"Not dangerous, as such. Well, no more than any of us." Edison made a back-and-forth, teeter-totter motion with his hand. "More...unstable. She doesn't see people as much, seeing as how she's in the middle of a giant labyrinth." He considered for a moment. "It's kind of like how Azrael radiates Death – she knows all paths and so no paths lead to her unless she wants them to. She bends them away."

Edison chuckled. "She's gone a bit crazy, though. You know that whole Bermuda triangle thing? Or the lost plane...who was that? The famous woman pilot?"

"Amelia Earhart?"

"Yeah! Her! Anyway, Despoina makes them get lost – or helps them find their way. If she decides to help us, then that Egg, if it exists, is just a hop, skip, and jump away. If she rejects us..."

"We end up trapped in a maze forever." Liara pursed her lips. "What made you go, when you did? What were you looking for?"

Edison rubbed the back of his neck, eyes shifting around. "Is it that important?"

Liara shrugged. "It might be. Helps to know how your comrade-in-arms works, how he thinks." Edison nodded, but still did not speak.

"Well?"

He put his hands up in a 'surrender' gesture. "All right, all right...tell you the truth, I was...looking for where my parents were buried."

Liara blinked. "What?"

Edison sighed, put his head in his hands. "You know how it was back in the Hellenic time period, when I had my Second Birth. My parents were academicians, scholars, and they wanted the same for me. When the call went out for soldiers to fight the Persians, I...I stood. I wanted to help my countrymen, to keep us free."

Edison's eyes came up, locking with Liara's, filled with tears. "We had a fight. A terrible fight...I called them cowards. I called my parents, the people who gave me life...cowards. I said they weren't worthy of the freedoms that the soldiers' lives buy for them." A sad, shameful chuckle. "Guess I forgot that those freedoms included the right to protest them." He shook his head. "So we fought, and then I left. I went with the army when it marched, and then I had my Second Birth..." The tears began to run down, pattering unheeded on the dirty bus floor between their shoes. "I never saw them again. At first it didn't matter. I was flush with the power, running wild with it, crossing continents we had never heard of before. It was wonderful, it was madness...and, eventually, it wore off. Eventually, I remembered them, remembered what I had done. I went looking for them...but I forgot how much time had passed. They were dead. My brothers and sister were dead. So were their children, and theirs." Edison waved his hands, his voice catching in his throat. Liara interrupted him.

"So you went to Despoina to find their

tombs, to say goodbye?"

"Something like that." Edison looked into Liara's eyes, questioning. "Is this the best we've got? Do we go?"

Liara leaned out of her seat. "Hey, Rob! Nearest airport; we've got a plane to catch!"

"Yes, ma'am!" Rob's blue eyes shined behind his glasses as he gunned the engine and shifted to the carpool lane. "Want me to call ahead?"

"Got it." Edison was grinning – now that a decision had been made, his color had risen.

Finally, we have something. Liara couldn't stop the smile from spreading across her face as well. *Something to shoot for. A path to travel. Let's go.*

11 – SEEKER IN THE CITY

Oreth almost didn't feel the pain.

The Woman's knives cut into his flesh as he lay, naked, on her table, coating it in his blood. When he opened his eyes, he saw raw, unadulterated joy in hers.

She reminded him of someone...who was it, again? Someone he was close to, once...

And then the fire burned the thought from his mind; he bit his tongue to keep from screaming, more of his blood pouring down his throat.

Oreth knew that his body *should* be dead – that even he, with the power in his soul, could not survive this.

He also knew why he was *not* dead. The man

(*thing, monster*)

in the corner of the room, who watched his torment with dispassionate eyes, would not let him die. Not until he had done what was promised, so long ago.

Oreth found this unfair – not just the torment, but the whole situation. He didn't even remember what the promise *was*, and Azrael wouldn't tell him, only saying that he was willing to wait as long as necessary for Oreth to come around.

Oreth opened his eyes again...but these were not his eyes, not really; his eyes were coated with blood, after all, but these looked out over the room, unfogged and unblinded. With the eyes of his mind, Oreth looked around.

He saw the Woman for who she was, now – Eriana, once his wife, his beloved, now delighting in the slow tearing of his flesh and the screams of his soul.

Why? What have I done to you? How did I...

As the feelings crossed through Oreth's mind, the echoes of Eriana's own thoughts came back to him.

Bastard! It's about time...after you left me, how could you leave me, I loved you! How could you! 'A god must not be held back by a mortal love?' Now I'm a god, you monster! Her eyes blazed once more. *Burn, fucker, burn!*

Another wound cauterized by the flames of the poker...but this one Oreth did not feel at all, only watched with a clinical air. He saw the auras around all three of them – Azrael, swathed in black shapes that screamed like children trapped in a burning building...but not burning themselves. Eriana, flashes of red blood, splashing, pouring, gushing, over and over, and screams of insane rage echoing from within her spirit, hiding flickers of light that struggled to break free. His own, guttering in the firelight, barely visible buildings, roadways, and crowds of people.

But there was something else here. Oreth turned his head to see.

There was a great door, golden, with light streaming through the edges and the keyhole. Oreth knew what this door was, and he was tempted to take it.

Then he saw Death.

Death, clad in its dark robes and skeletal hands, stood in front of the door, arms crossed.

There is *a Grim Reaper.* Oreth's thoughts were filled with wonder. *If there is a Death...what* else *have we missed?*

Oreth walked to it, his steps easy and light. "Will you let me pass?"

The figure shook its head. *No.*

"Why not?"

For a moment, no answer. Oreth felt his body tug at him, pulling him back, but he held his ground. "Why not?" He struggled to stay where he was, digging his feet into the ground. "Let me go! Let me die!"

Death pulled its hands out of its robes, and dangling from its bony fingers, connecting them like a gilded chain, were two amulets, black and gold, carved with runes. Names.

One read: Oreth, holder of the Nature of Cities.

The other: Azrael, holder of the Nature of

Death.

And it shook its head again. *No.*

Oreth opened his mouth to speak, but before the words could leave his throat he was jerked back, as if he were tied to a jet airplane as it took off, dragging him behind. This sensation persisted for a few seconds...and then he was back in his body, screaming and crying with renewed agony.

"Enough, Eriana." Azrael touched her shoulder. Eriana turned on him, eyes murderous and flooded with tears, teeth clenched. Her chest rose and fell with her rapid breaths, and she bared her teeth at Azrael like an animal interrupted during feeding time. Azrael stared her down, unmoving, until she backed off.

Oreth almost managed a smile. He had an idea.

Azrael came forward and leaned close, his dark eyes boring into Oreth's. "Why are you doing this, old friend?"

Oreth laughed at the absurdity of the question. The laugh hurt.

"Last time...I checked," he managed, "I wasn't the one...with the knife."

Azrael did not smile. "You promised me,

once, that you would...help me."

"Help you?" Oreth rolled his eyes. "Sure...let me...get out...my checkbook."

Azrael cocked his head, and Oreth saw his face curl up, his brows knit together.

He's confused.

"Go." Azrael turned his profile to Eriana. She was glaring at Oreth's mauled body, and did not move at first. When Azrael repeated his command, she started, and drew herself up.

She stood her ground.

Azrael's eyes held hers for a few seconds, then he turned back toward his captive.

"Two thousand years ago, you promised to link your Nature to mine. Death has consumed me; it follows everywhere I walk and decimates those whom I meet."

"I...noticed."

Azrael continued without acknowledging Oreth's interruption. "By linking our Natures, the...excessive portion of mine would express itself through yours.

Oreth' tried to sit up, the agony forgotten, as his eyes widened. "W...what did you say?"

Azrael's voice marched on. "Cities would become receptacles for Death. The mortals in those cities would experience a...shift...in the birth rate vs. death rate equilibrium. Over time, population growth would cease in those cities."

"You mean there would be the widespread genocide of millions, possibly billions, of human beings?"

Azrael shook his head. "Genocide is far too harsh, Oreth." He held his two hands out in front of him, representing a scale. "This would simply make life a little more dangerous; a 5% increase in traffic accidents, for instance, or lethal electrical malfunctions. Your Nature is large enough to absorb the excess of mine without self-destructing, you see." Azrael paced the room. "It's not as if you are the first Essential whom I have enlisted for this. The world has not ended yet, Oreth. I doubt very much that it would just because I joined my Nature to yours."

"And...why the hell would I agree to this?"

Azrael sighed, a parent explaining things to a child. "Because the alternative is for me to kill you and find the next person the Nature passes to." A thin smile touched Azrael's lips. "I imagine that person would be...cooperative."

Part of Oreth's being, a deep, scared part,

screamed at him

(*I can't die no I must live*)

to accept Azrael's offer, to accede, to avoid death at all costs.

"All right." Oreth dropped his eyes from Azrael. "I have one condition."

Azrael cocked his head again, searching over Oreth's face.

"Yes?"

"Give me the girl's life."

"Why?"

Oreth's voice dropped further. "To heal myself. If I am to live, I would like to be whole."

Azrael curved an eyebrow as Eriana hissed.

"Very well." In his hands Azrael produced the shimmering, shifting globe that represented Liara's life force, and laid it on Oreth's chest. The wounded Essential took hold of the power.

"You plan to let him live? To let him go?" Eriana's fists were clenched, and she spat her words at the other..

Azrael glanced her way. "Yes. Is that a problem?"

"Yes! You promised! He betrayed me! I demand vengeance!" Color rose in Eriana's face; a face that Oreth had loved once, a face that was beautiful and would still be so, if it were not etched with such rage.

Azrael said something in reply, but Oreth had turned his mind inward. He reached out to the life on his chest, both with his mind and with his hand. He felt the raw power beating within, the essence of Life, the Life of an Essential, fierce, strong, and tempered like the Forge it had been born on.

In the recesses of his mind, another memory, pulled, it seemed, from the very mists by the touch of this essence against his chest, awoke. The raw power beating became a heart, the warmth was a chest pressed against his. Two bodies connected in the ancient dance that served to connect the souls as well, and he could feel her soul, Liara's soul, yearning to be joined to his as their bodies were.

And he felt his own deep indifference, the knowledge that this was a purely physical act, mutual masturbation, no more.

Nothing more. His heart bled as he saw the hope and desire in her eyes for the first time in the window of memory. *I'm so sorry that I didn't see it before.* The memory faded, but the guilt, the shame, remained.

Oreth flexed his strength – he thanked whatever God there may be that Azrael was distracted – and connected the life essence to his own. He felt the joining, a conduit forming between them, such as had never happened before.

And, in a convulsive burst of force, he threw both of them away. He laughed.

Azrael turned, his eyes filled with a fury Oreth had never seen in that calm face. The stone under his white shoes split and the air warped with his rage.

It was satisfying.

Now merely human, no longer bound against entering the gates, Oreth spat in the face of Death before it claimed him.

INTERLUDE

Azrael's distress was apparent on his face as Oreth's body crumbled before his eyes.

He's...IT'S gone. I found it and it's gone.

The thought repeated itself again and again.

"He sent it away." He sat down and ran his hand through his hair. "How did he do that? How did he manage that?"

"You know he sent it to his bitch." Eriana stepped up next to him. "We can find her." She smiled a slight, barely-there smile, and went on: "I'll enjoy finding her."

"You think so?" Azrael stood, then rounded on Eriana, screaming in her face, his eyes bloodshot and his veins distended, the force of his rage shoving her into the wall. Her impact cracked the stone.

"SHE HAS BOTH THEIR NATURES NOW, YOU FUCKING CUNT! IT TOOK YOU OVER A THOUSAND YEARS TO FIND HIM AGAIN; HOW THE HELL DO YOU EXPECT TO FIND HER?"

The onslaught, verbal and metaphysical, left Eriana speechless and on the verge of tears.

Azrael took a deep breath to calm himself. "I did not anticipate that he would sacrifice himself for her." He clenched his fist, brought the knuckle to his lips. "This is not something he would have done before."

He turned to Eriana. "Find her. Bring her to me. We will carve the Nature out of her soul, if we must."

Eriana's face quavered for a moment. She closed her eyes, took two breaths, opened them and nodded.

"As you wish."

~~~

Oreth, the Essential of Cities, he who rode forth to protect Rome from Alaric and the Visigoth invasion...was dying.

He dropped to one knee as his strength evaporated; the sword which Liara had forged for him fell from his hand, and he braced himself on the ground. There was an outcry from the Roman soldiers, and bless them, they charged, rallying to his defense.

They were trying to save him. Mortal men trying to save a god. Even in the throes of his death-agony, Oreth laughed. Then he cried, his tears running out of the visor covering his face.

He thought he heard someone calling his name, crying out for him. It didn't matter. His muscles could no longer hold him. He collapsed to the ground, but his mind refused to still.

"No! I can't die! Mortals die, normal things die, not gods! Not I! No! I refuse!"

All of his refusal was irrelevant, of course.

Through the water in his eyes, Oreth
~~~

could see a figure advancing. A very dark man, darker than even himself, striding through the battlefield unseen. His white robes were immaculate, even in the chaos of the combat.

"Azrael." He breathed the name.

"Azrael."

PART TWO

12 – MISTRESS OF THE LABYRINTH

Liara and Edison stepped out of the gleaming white Heraklion International Airport into the bright morning sun of the island of Crete. The Mediterranean air was salty and warm, and Liara's red hair danced around her like a flame. She pulled her wrap more tightly around her body.

"Good day for a quest!" Edison stretched out his arms, then put on his sunglasses to shield his eyes from the glare before sipping his latte. "It's too bad I don't have a suit of armor and my trusty steed with me."

"I could fix the armor, Edison." Liara elbowed him in the ribs. "But I don't know if Rob would appreciate being called your 'trusty steed.'"

Edison did a spit-take, spewing his latte out on the sidewalk. He wiped his face as he stared at Liara.

"I didn't think you had it in you!"

Liara shrugged, smiling, and looked out over the landscape. A modern city had sprung up here, but as with many places in the Old World, there were still remnants of the civilizations that had come before; new homes built with old bricks, as it were. Ancient rubbed shoulders with modern in this place; this was one of many things which the Essentials could identify with.

"Where do we go, Edison?" Her eyes panned over the landscape. "Where is Despoina?"

"Oh...right, well, we need to head to Knossos." Seeing Liara's blank look, he added, "It was the palace of King Minos, and, in the myths, the site of the Labyrinth." He laughed. "Where were you when this was going on?"

"I haven't had as much time as I would like to brush up on the classics; *some* of us actually do work, you know." She smiled. "Which way?"

Edison pointed down a wide street, and the two of them began walking. It wound through tightly-packed houses on either side. Residents called to people they saw in the road, friends exchanging greetings and how-dos.

The air was calm and peaceful as the pair of Essentials passed through the crowds. Edison's voice filled the airtime, talking about his previous visits, what had changed since the last one, and what some of the highlights were.

Liara, however, was busy with her own thoughts.

Something...something is wrong. Her eyes danced, not seeing anything. *I hear something, something I haven't heard before, in my soul...I hear the steel, the fires, but there's more.*

What is it?

Liara stretched her mind inward, but she

could make no sense of what she was hearing – it was like a foreign language to her. Murmurs whispered just under her ability to discern them, and strange images floated across the surface of her mind.

The traffic light turned green as they stepped into the street. The white walking man beckoned the crowds even as the opposing reds brought the cross traffic to a sudden stop. Liara barely noticed that anything had changed.

Then she glanced up.

The white walking man was not white at all, but red; it was the deep, crimson red of freshly spilled blood. Liara's eyes widened, and her gaze flickered, the panicked look of the animal caught in the trap.

Everyone around her, just for a moment, was also covered in blood. Blood they did not see or feel. Liara felt a great sense of sadness permeating the air, as if she were at a funeral for a beloved world leader or grandparent.

Then it was gone.

Gods, something is *wrong. What? What?*

Liara wasn't sure, and that fact drew deep lines across her brow. She forced her feet to keep walking,

Time passed and feet moved; the pair passed by street-side shops, angry debaters discussing politics, newspapers discussing the latest Grecian austerity measures, and several taverns whose open windows disgorged boisterous drinking songs. Liara was no longer keeping track of where she was, simply staying close to Edison while lost in her own

(*what is wrong it feels like him but different*)

considerations.

Edison poked her in the ribs to get her attention, and she started.

"You totally didn't hear a word I said, did you?"

Liara blinked. "Of course! I was..." She stopped, then laughed and shook her head. "No, I wasn't. Sorry."

Edison shrugged. "I was just saying that myself, actually. I'm sorry about earlier, on the bus."

It took Liara a moment to process what he was saying, to make the connection. "Oh. Well, you don't have to –"

"Yes, I do." His customary levity vanished. "You asked me to respect your privacy, and I didn't. That was an asinine thing to do, and I totally deserved that punch in the face." He extended a hand. "So, I'm sorry, Liara."

She smiled and shook it. "Thank you, Edison. I appreciate that. It means a lot to me."

Edison's smile leapt back onto his face, and they resumed their trek. A few minutes more and Edison put a hand on Liara's shoulder.

"Here we are, your majesty." He swept his arms before him like a performer taking a bow.

Liara's eyes fell upon a series of ruins, mere suggestions of where a grand palace must have stood...yes...here would have been a courtyard, now crumbled and decayed; here, a dining room, or ballroom perhaps, remarkable in size, but with most of its stone long since salvaged and scavenged for other purposes. Scattered and used, she thought, but the echoes are still here, and sometimes echoes were all one needed to find one's way.

"How do we get her attention?" Liara kept her voice low so as not to draw the attention of the tourists and visitors to the site. "Do we have to wait until nightfall, or what?"

Edison smiled and shook his head. "See that?" He pointed at a broken-down marble column. "That's the entrance to the Labyrinth. All we have to do is head down there and ask if she will let us in."

"Will she?"

"No telling. There are a couple of good signs, though."

"What're those?"

"She called us, for one, and we actually made it here, for the other. If she really, *really* didn't want to see us, or was trying to play a trick on us, we would be trapped in some sort of infinite loop, or be locked away in an alternate dimension, or something."

Liara smiled, then her eyes widened with fear and she grabbed Edison's arm. "Edison...are you sure we're not? Could she trap us in, I don't know, an illusion or something? Make us think that we're progressing when we're stuck?"

Edison tilted his head, considering, then shook it. "No. We're safe."

"How do you know?"

"I checked. I used the GPS satellites to make sure that we're really where we're supposed to be." He pointed up at the sky. "I don't know if she can do that or not, but one thing she *can't* do is confuse my powers directly. Or yours, for what that's worth. We're good."

Liara nodded, a weight lifting from her shoulders. "Great." She sighed. "Thanks, Edison."

Edison beamed his bright smile. "You're welcome."

The two of them approached the pillar. It was weather-beaten and worn, but Liara could still make out a carving – a double-headed axe, about one hand-span in width. Underneath was an inscription, in Greek:

<<For the Gods, honey.

For the Mistress of the Labyrinth, honey.>>

"Ah, shit!" Edison clapped his hand over his mouth after his exclamation, looking around to see if they had been noticed. "I forgot the damn honey. We need honey." He slapped himself on the forehead. "Figures I'd forget something."

"Why honey?"

"It's part of the legend, and Despoina plays the part to the hilt. It's why she uses that particular name. She won't even consider a request unless you offer her honey."

"Oh, no problem!" Liara said with her voice bright. "Oh, wait; darn...there aren't any places here to *get* honey, Edison."

"We'll just have to head back into town and see if we can pick some up." Edison's eyes were lowered. "I'm really sorry, Liara. I just didn't remember; it's been a long time."

Liara sighed. 'It's okay, Edison; I know it was an accident. But we're running out of *time*; Azrael could finish with Oreth and then, well..." She shook her head. "I just wish that we didn't have to go hunting that honey down..."

As she finished her sentence, Liara's vision went blurry and she almost lost her balance. A sound like a far-off call, a summons, echoed in her ears.

"What?" Something deep *pulled* within her – the feeling brought back memories of her Second Birth, when she had tried to master her new power – and a big, long, blue-and-white city bus labeled ANTELOPE VALLEY TRANSIT AUTHORITY pulled up from nowhere; eyewitnesses later would swear that there had been no bus anywhere in sight before it had appeared. The crowd of tourists erupted in conversation, and security officers ran to the bus and pounded on the door, some drawing their weapons. The driver opened it, her eyes wide with fright.

<<What are you doing here? Step out of the bus at once!>>

"What are you saying?" The bus driver, an elderly black woman, was on the verge of tears, eyes dancing back and forth in her panic. "What's going on? Where the hell am I?"

Liara stared at the scene, looked at Edison, then stared again. Finally, she forced her feet to move and walked to the bus.

<Um..ma'am?>> One of the security guards reached out, putting a meaty hand on Liara's shoulder. <<We have...a situation here, and you should wait until we've figured this out.>>

<<Gregoris,>> Liara began, <<it's all right.>> The security guard blinked, and Liara realized what she had just said. *I know his name.* Then, in the next breath: *I know* <u>him.</u>

This security guard was part of her, just as stone and metal were the products of the Forge.

Because he belonged to the City.

She stumbled backward. *Oh, Gods...Oreth. What happened to you?*

<<...Ma'am?>> The voice of the guard came again.

Liara shook her head, brought her eyes to Gregoris'...and *pushed*. <<Let us pass,>>

<<Of course, Mistress Liara. Go right ahead.>> The guards moved aside, tipping their hats as she went. They resumed their work once she had gone, and never gave the two Essentials a second look.

Edison walked with Liara for a few paces past the security, onto the bus filled with con-fused American passengers, and then turned to her. "How did you do that?" His lips barely moved as he spoke. "You don't have power over security guards, do you?"

"Later." Liara shook her head. "Right now, we need to find the honey." She raised her voice and addressed the passengers, who looked up at her as she began speaking. "Does anyone have any honey we could buy?" The passengers' conversations rose in volume. *Honey? Is this some kind of prank T.V. show or something?* A few titters of laughter rose up from the back of the bus.

"It is actually very important." Her eyes were earnest, pleading. "I would be most grateful if you could help."

The inter-passenger discussions continued for a few more moments, individual words lost in a sea of mumbled consonants. Finally, an ancient-looking man in blacks and greys stood and adjusted his glasses. "I don't know what this is about, miss, but my folks taught me to know when someone is in trouble." His lined face crinkled into a smile. "You look to me to be in trouble."

He dug into his knapsack, pulling out a small jar of clover honey. Organic.

"I keep it for m'health." He stepped out and placed it in Liara's outstretched hand. "One spoon with every meal keeps things workin', young lady." The man dropped her a wink.

Liara took a ring off of her left hand. It had alternating gold and silver bands, cerulean sapphires that caught and reflected the lighting, and the inside of the ring was engraved with ancient runes describing long life and vigor.

She took one of the old man's swollen, arthritic hands in hers and slipped the ring onto one of his fingers, whispering softly as she did so.

"Hey there, miss! I think I'm just a bit old for ya!" The man laughed, and Liara smiled.

."I think you'll find this to be even better for your health than a spoonful of honey. Thank you." She kissed his forehead. The man's smile broadened, and he went back to his seat, with that smile leading the way.

Edison raised his hands and waited for a moment while the voices around him settled.

"Welcome to Crete." A shout of protest erupted from the passengers, and Edison waved his hands until they settled. "We'll be getting you out of here as soon as we can." He smiled. "It might be best if you just...took a nap, and hopefully, when you wake up, this will all be over."

"Is this some kind of crazy government experiment?" shouted a voice from the back of the bus.

"Are we on T.V.?" called another.

Edison seemed to consider this, hand on his chin, then grinned again. He looked from side to side. "Definitely not. NO." He nodded his head *yes*. "No way would the government do something like this. No way. No how."

Liara grabbed his arm at the elbow and began pulling him away, but Edison continued, "Remember, kids: your government is your *friend*!"

Then Liara tossed him off the bus, nodded at the wide-eyed driver, and stepped out.

"Government conspiracies? Seriously, Edison?"

He shrugged, still laughing. "Hey, if you can't have fun while risking your immortal existence, what's the point, right?" The smile dropped off his face. "Well...I guess it's time to see if the Lady will see us." A hard swallow. "Let's go, Liara."

Liara was already halfway to the marble column which was supposed to anchor the Labyrinth. She turned and looked back over her shoulder with a smile.

"Move it, Edison, or I'll leave you here, and you'll miss the dangerous, death-defying journey into the labyrinth. You don't want to lose this chance to die horribly, do you?"

"Oh!" Edison slapped his forehead with the heel of his hand. "What was I worried about? Let's do this, then!" He charged after her, taking her hand as he caught up.

The two ran towards the pillar, laughing

with the exertion, and Liara realized that she was having *fun*. It made no sense – Azrael was angry at them, Oreth was likely dead or about to be...but then maybe that was it. Maybe it was the danger, the fear, that made the rest of it better.

Maybe she was laughing to keep herself from crying. Or maybe it was something else.

The column stood before them like a spear thrown by the Gods and imbedded into the ground; a thunderbolt of Zeus, perhaps, pinning the reality of this world to another. There was another world here, yes; Liara could feel that strange "doubling" that she always encountered when near such a nexus, as if her thoughts were echoing in her mind and her words bouncing in the air.

All one needed to do was open the door.

Liara handed the honey to Edison. She stepped back and bowed her head.

"Make your magic."

Edison twisted the lid of the jar open and dipped his finger, bringing out a large glob of sweet syrup. By now, a few people had gathered, looking on, wondering what they were doing.

<<Honey for the Gods,>> Edison used the honey to draw the circular sigil which was the symbol of the Olympian pantheon of deities. He dipped his finger again.

<<Honey for the Mistress,>> Now he traced the double-headed axe carving, leaving glistening honey in the crevices. He poured a small amount onto the ground, then dropped the jar and took Liara's hand in his own.

For several seconds, nothing happened. Liara could feel her heartbeat quickening. *Is she ignoring us? Testing us?*

She opened her mouth to ask Edison if it normally took this long, when she felt it, like a vibrating string in her brain.

The honey offered to the Olympians dissipated, floating on the air like flower petals. The honey for Despoina, however, thickened and began to course down the monument, pooling in great puddles on the ground beneath the column.

<<What the hell?>> Members of the crowd began to exclaim in wonder and panic..

The honey gushed from the labrys, the double-axe, until the pools of honey on the ground resembled a small lake, clover smell permeating the air.

An image appeared in the honey: a beautiful woman, dark of hair and eye, and dressed in the Classical Greek toga and headdress. With both hands, she beckoned, and her lips voiced a single word.

Come.

The two Essentials held each other's eyes and hands for about three seconds...and then they stepped into the pool.

INTERLUDE

"Goodbye, my love."

Oreth kissed his wife's hand, grasped the trowel that was his symbol of power and office in his own, and then closed his eyes.

As she watched, he vanished, leaving her in their palace, tears streaming, agony within her heart.

"He is gone!" The gathered subjects began to murmur, voices rising. "The god is gone!"

She turned to the crowd, her eyes flicking from one face to the next. The men and women stared at the empty seat.

Then their focus shifted.

Angry voices rang out. Accusations. Threats.

"He was unnatural, a devil!" "Thank the gods he's gone!" "Now we can live in peace without him looking over our shoulders."

Then one broke the general din. "What if he comes back?"

The dark-haired Queen took a step back, her hand clutching the back of the bronze throne.

Someone pointed at her.

"She can summon him!" The crowd turned. "We've seen her do it!"

Her mind flooded with fear, the primal emotion merging with the grief, the loss.

She was paralyzed.

When they swarmed toward her, she did not run.

When their hands grasped her, she did not fight.

When they cut off her clothes with their knives, she did not beg.

When they raped her on the floor of her throne room, she did not scream.

When they came, finally, to kill her, she gave herself over to Vengeance.

And not one of them survived it.

~~~

Eriana stepped out from behind the bus, watching as Liara

(*the bitch*)

and the other one vanished into the Labyrinth, sinking down into the honey lake, which crystallized, dried up, and blew away as soon as they had disappeared.

Eriana ran her hands through her dark hair, her nostrils flaring.

Why are they here? What do they want from her? What could they be looking for?

So far, it looked like the bitch didn't know Oreth had sent her his power...his Nature. It was there, for certain; Eriana could taste its presence on the air like ozone after a lightning strike. Perhaps she didn't realize he was dead yet.

This thought brought her up short. Azrael had been right about one thing – Oreth wouldn't have made this kind of sacrifice be-
~~~

fore; he had always had too keen a sense of his own safety, too much love for his own immortality.

It must have been true. The realization was painful to her, pulling at her heart. *Even though I didn't believe him. He must have forgotten...forgotten everything.* Her breath left her body in one long exhalation.

Where does that leave me?

For Eriana, whose nature was Vengeance, the act of betrayal was ever fresh and never healing; she felt the agony of her heart breaking each moment, as if it were the first.

Her eyes fell on the "misplaced" bus, where the passengers were trying to communicate with the security, some rifling through their suitcases for phrasebooks and dictionaries to get points across.

She

(*the bitch*)

had done this, yes, but she had seemed as surprised as anyone. Maybe...and she shook her head. No, it didn't matter; betrayal is betrayal, she reminded herself, and betrayal must be repaid.

In blood.

<<Excuse me, miss; do you have a cigarette?>> A well-dressed, middle-aged Greek man with thinning hair approached the Essential. He laughed, <<I haven't smoked in 12 years, but today seems like...well, seems like I need one, you know?>>

Eriana's Nature boiled; this man was a traitor. He had betrayed his wife,

(no honey I was working late at the office)

betrayed his children,

(Daddy you promised never to touch me like that again)

and betrayed himself.

(Just once more I won't ever take it again but I need it just once)

Eriana reached under the neckline of her dress and produced a cigarette. Taking it, the man smelled and examined the gift. He looked at Eriana and smiled.

<<What kind is this?>>

<<A very special brand,>> A lighter appeared in her hand. <<*Athalaxa.*>>

The man bent his head, rose with a lit cigarette and a smile. <<Smooth flavor.>> He nodded to her and began to walk away. <Thank you!>>

Eriana smiled, seeing the mark of the curse she had laid on the man form on his forehead.

<<You're quite welcome.>>

13 – LINGERING IN THE LABYRINTH

There is no doubt about it. Liara stood staring at the vast expanse before her. *The Labyrinth is* epic.

Her first impression was that the Labyrinth was a giant three-dimensional maze, spherical in shape, suspended in the air by purplish beams of energy which appeared to come from nowhere. There were sliding walls and hidden doorways, and moss coated many of the surfaces. From her vantage point at the top of the path leading down towards the great maze, however, she realized that the maze did not have three dimensions at all; it had four; there were distortions, warps in the light as it reflected off different sections of the maze caused by changes in the speed of the rays.

When she mentioned this, Edison nodded.

"Sometimes you'll find tracks that you haven't left yet, or trigger a switch that does something you've already seen." He sobered, the amusement and joviality leaving his voice. "Or you can pull a 'Back to the Future' and end up somewhere else, somewhere you've been."

"Is it possible to...meet yourself?"

He shook his head. "Never heard of that happening, although it would be interesting, wouldn't it?" He paused to let her catch up with him. "I've never bumped into myself either, for what that's worth."

"How many times have you been down here?"

"Once."

"So, not exactly a comprehensive test, then?"

Edison shrugged. "I've also made it out once, which is one more time than most people."

Liara squared her shoulders and began walking down the clear dirt path, Edison a half-step behind her. Her head moved on a swivel, prepared for threats.

The staircase up to the floating Labyrinth was grey flagstone, heavy, dense, and littered with skeletons – some whole, most not – and she opened the small, oaken door leading inward.

The other side of the opening was dark.

Liara and Edison stepped through.

The path seemed to stretch on forever, curving in one direction or another, but never actually swerving at all. The sky

(*what the fuck how is there a sky?*)

was changing color, from blue to pink, as if sunrise was reversing itself.

After two or three hours of this wandering, Liara rubbed her hand across her eyes, wiping the fatigue out of them, pausing for a moment to massage the bridge of her nose. Her hand left her face and her lids came up. The sunlight dazzled her, warm, rich, and yellow. She blinked, letting herself adjust to the sudden increase in light.

"Edison?" There was no answer; figures began to blur into sight, resolving into...a farm? Three or four buildings, green grass across lush fields, a handmade see-saw underneath a sprawling willow tree...and two figures, one large and one small, standing near a small stream that cut through the landscape. Liara's heart leapt and began to beat faster as the larger of the figures hoisted the smaller onto its shoulders.

The smaller figure cried out in glee, a high-pitched, giggly sound, as the larger began to spin around. Liara took a hesitant step forward, her mouth forming a word, something to say, but her words were drowned out by the call from the farm door. A red-haired woman - statuesque, marked by sun with freckles splayed over her cheeks - shouted across the field.

"Terry! Liara! It's time for lunch!" As the door closed, a clay pot perched on the window-sill fell over and shattered.

Liara's eyes began to stream with tears, the small smile she had worn vanishing in an instant as she began to walk, then to run, toward the two figures hurrying home, the little girl laughing, bouncing on her father's shoulders as he glanced up at his red-haired daughter.

"Wait!" She ran faster. "Stop! You need to…" She found herself unable to look away, unable to keep her eyes off of this thing that was about to happen, unable to tear herself from the tragedy ahead.

It happened in slow motion – the leather boot of the father sank into a sinkhole; the smile on his face vanished as he realized his predicament, then turned into a grimace-becoming-scream as he began to pitch forward.

Liara's hand covered her mouth as she saw her younger self grab onto her father's head in fear, her red hair streaming past her pale face as she fell. The sound from the screams began to echo in Liara's ears, but she did not register it, too busy watching and reliving the scene playing itself out before her eyes.

Her father began to spin, reaching up as he did so to cradle his daughter in his arms. The loud *snap* of his ankle cracking jarred Liara from her fascinated stare, and she resumed her run toward the two.

The pair thudded into the ground; the girl was thrown from her father's arms to roll in the dirt, coming up crying; the father, however, did not move, did not scream any more.

The younger Liara crawled toward her stricken father and hugged his flopping head to her chest, as the elder one arrived and stood over the scene. The little girl kissed her father's forehead; blood flowed over her dress, her legs, her hands from the huge gash in the back of his head, staining her skin and the grass crimson.

"Da." She pushed his shoulder, trying to rouse him. "Wake up, Da. Wake up." She turned her head toward the house, tears flowing from her eyes. "Ma! Da's hurt! Ma!"

Liara reached out to her younger self, trying to think of something to say to comfort the child, while holding back the renewed emotions streaming forth from the forgotten depths of her heart. The girl hadn't even noticed her yet, alternating between holding her father's stricken head and yelling for her mother. Liara glanced up at the farm door; her mother was going to burst through it in a few seconds, but she couldn't bring herself to leave. She began to bend down toward the sobbing child.

A hand grasped her shirt, pulled her backward.

Liara spun around, heart picking up speed, ready to strike whoever it was; her fist lashed out in reflex toward the head she glimpsed out of the corner of her eye.

The fist sank into solid, luminescent stone. It buried itself to the wrist.

Edison was crouched on the floor of the Labyrinth, eyes darting from the fist to Liara's face and back again, before Liara removed her hand. The two were still for several seconds before Edison spoke.

"Ummm...was it me or the wall you were mad at?" He turned toward the crater, then back, one corner of his mouth upturned.

Liara's red, tear-streaked face stretched; her mouth quivered.

Then she smiled. Laughed. Cried. Laughed and cried some more as she pulled her fist out of the wall and sank to the ground, resting her head in her crossed arms. Edison got to his knees and touched her on the arm.

"Hey." He put one finger under her chin and lifted her face to look at him. "You okay?"

Liara's voice, thick and stuffy from her crying, emerged from the encirclement of her limbs. "No, Edison, I'm not okay. Not okay at all."

Edison nodded and sat back on his haunches, waiting.

Liara's crying stretched out for a few moments more, than began to subside, becoming sobs, then hitches, then sniffles. She raised her head and looked at Edison. His eyes were wide and wary as they searched her face, looking for any hint of further aggression.

She nodded and smiled at him, and he relaxed.

"I guess you were wrong about that whole 'not meeting yourself' thing, Edison." She lowered her head again and gave a sad little laugh.

"What happened?" His eyes were saucers, glowing in the strange blue-purple light from the Labyrinth walls.

She shook her head. "It's not that important. It was just a very sad memory, one that I've always felt was my fault, even though it wasn't, you know?"

Edison nodded. "I have a few of those as well, Liara." There was a moment of silence as he looked around at the maze surrounding them. "Interesting that it sent you somewhere you were already at. It raises questions."

Liara scrunched her face, confused. "What questions?"

Edison stood and began to pace. "Well, what would have happened if you had changed...wait." He stopped in his tracks and turned towards Liara again. "You *didn't* change anything, did you?"

She shook her head, and he continued. "Okay, so what would have happened if you had? Would we remember what *had* been, and be on a different timeline, for example, or would we just remember the way things were after you had changed them? Would you re-member things one way and me the other? What about the rest of the world...?" Edison went on in this vein for several minutes, postu-lating and hypothesizing, until Liara stood.

"We should get going, Edison." She wiped the last of the tears from her eyes. "We don't have a lot of time, and I don't know how much we've lost."

Edison grimaced. "You're right; it's almost impossible to tell how much time has gone by when you're in a place where time is, well..." and he scratched his neck, "...irrelevant, I sup-pose." He looked right, then left, then right again. Suddenly, he made a sweeping bow at the waist, gesturing with his arms to the left-most pathway.

"I suppose we should press on, then? After you, mademoiselle."

~~~

Time passed. The two Essentials climbed and descended staircases, pulled their way up vine-covered walls, and searched out secret passages on their trek towards the center of the great Labyrinth, and Despoina, Keeper of the Ways.

Liara put a hand on Edison's shoulder. "Are we even going the right way?"

Edison laughed. "You're saying that like there *is* a right way. The Labyrinth changes all the time – that's just part of its charm."

"Why does Despoina do this?" Liara rubbed her upper arms. "Why live in a place..." she paused, looking around at the strangeness of the landscape. "...like this?"

"Step up on the wall."

Seeing Liara's wide-eyed stare, Edison said, "Like this," and planted his foot onto the adjacent wall. With a sudden shift of weight, he
~~~

stood horizontal to Liara, his face near hers.

After a moment of looking at his eyes, she stepped back. "How did you do that?"

Another laugh. "Gravity's subjective here. Basically, as long as you're *on* a path, you can *walk* the path." He pointed forward/up, and Liara saw an opening in the...the sky? It looked like a tunnel entrance.

How is there a tunnel in the sky? She stepped up to the wall and placed a foot on it. "So...I just...walk?"

Edison's smile glinted in the fading sunlight. "First time...well, only time...that I came here, I had to walk down a path that was spiraling around an octagonal pillar. It kept flipping over itself, looping..." He laughed. "Couldn't find my way out for hours. Turns out I had to walk backwards. Got past it in twenty seconds flat after that." Liara's look stopped him. "Anyway, yes; you just have to walk, Liara."

Liara raised her left foot. For a moment, she was swept up in vertigo, feeling like she was caught between two worlds, a child with her feet over an edge but no way to pull herself back up. She closed her eyes, but that only made it worse.

"Liara!" came Edison's voice. "Pick a direction! Don't just hang out there in the middle!"

Liara heard this as if Edison was down a long, deserted hallway, his words bouncing off the walls.

I'm falling, Da! Something inside her was screaming. *Help!*

The fear that thought engendered was paralyzing, just as it had paralyzed the child who had experienced it.

A hand pressed into hers. Liara's eyes opened to see Edison looking into them.

"Take the step, Liara."

Liara's left foot came down on the wall, and the feeling, that feeling that a terrible, terrible fall was unavoidable, vanished at once. The echoes of memory faded with it.

The two of them stood like that for a few more moments, hand in hand.

His eyes. Like I can see into his soul...so deep...

The corners around those eyes crinkled a little. "You alright?" Edison's voice had returned to normal, his customary tone reemerging.

Liara blushed and nodded, releasing his

hand.

"You first."

Edison bowed, looked up, smiled. He turned to the entrance and called, "Despoina? Are you home?"

His voice resounded down the tunnel, repeating echoes fading with time. The two proceeded down the twists and turns of the Labyrinth and, for Liara, it started to become a game. They would bound from one side of the tunnel to another, or run circles around each other on the walls. They climbed up the sides of staircases and crawled on the bottoms of slides. After some time

(*how long?*)

Edison tapped her on the back, yelling, "You're It!" and running down the hallway at breakneck speed. Liara began to give chase...but she brought herself up short.

Something was wrong.

(*Don't stop come play!*)

Edison looked

(*Go get him have* fun!)

different.

What is it?

"Hey, Liara, come on! What're you waiting

for?" Edison's light, boyish voice beckoned her.

His voice is different too. What is going…

Then it hit her.

"Edison!" Fear flooded her brain. "Stop! Come back!"

By now, Edison was almost out of view. "Last one's a rotten egg!"

"Edison!" She waved at him, beckoning him back…then stopped, staring at her fingers. Her hand had become delicate and pale…and small.

Like it had never touched a hammer or anvil.

Like it had looked when she was a child.

"We're turning younger, Edison! You need to come back!"

No response. She could no longer see him.

"EDISON!" Her call, closer to a scream, echoed. She thought she heard something, but the sound

(*cry*)

was unintelligible.

Liara sat and began rummaging, digging through that Otherspace she called her "toolbox." The rings on her fingers and her bracelets slid over her skin, far too large for her current body.

How long do I have? Panic threatened to overwhelm her, but she forced it down as she searched. Finding what she was looking for – a great rope forged from metals which could drive a chemical engineer to suicide – she pulled it out of the Otherspace.

Have to hurry. Liara focused her power to engrave runes upon the rope, to bind it to her Nature and to her will. The power was slow in coming, as if it was far away, and it seemed an eternity before the cord was prepared to follow her commands. She whispered and the rope fell to the ground, slithering into the darkness.

Would the magic of this place affect her arts? Liara simply didn't know. Her protective jewelry seemed functional, which was a good sign, but this was sorcery like she had never encountered before.

No wonder nobody visits Despoina. She's a bitch.

The sinuous sound of the rope had faded, leaving Liara in the silence. She was tempted to shout, to bang on the walls, to make *some* noise to defeat the oppressive quiet which assaulted her senses with its sheer NOT-ness.

She did not, however; something else *felt* wrong, felt scarier than the silence.

After a great deal of time, (five minutes? Five hours? Who could know, here?) Liara heard the slithering again, but it felt heavier, and there was kind of a "thump" every few seconds. Her heart rose a little.

The rope came into the lit area, dragging an unconscious child with it.

Edison looked about twelve or thirteen — the shadow of the man he would

(*is!*)

become on his face, but the innocence and freedom of a child still present. Something was still missing, but Liara could not place what it was.

Liara's fingers grazed his cheek. *When did I last look like that? When did any of us?*

Liara was lost in thought for a few moments, then she started. "Shit," she said, and stretched out her fingers again.

The rings did not look any larger on her hands. Liara breathed a sigh.

So maybe it's not time spent here, but...distance? Maybe if we go back?

A few whispered incantations got the rope

moving again, pulling Edison behind her as she turned the way they had come.

The way was blocked. A solid flagstone wall stretched across their entire path, stretching up into the infinite sky, standing as a monument of impermeability.

Liara sank to her knees. "What am I supposed to do now?" She began to cry, her tears making small craters in the dust by her hands. She found it hard to get a grip on her emotions; her discipline, learned from centuries of patient forging, seemed to have deserted her. "Can't go back, can't go forward..." Her words came out almost singsong, and part of her wondered if she was losing her mind. She shook her head.

"Fuck that shit." She clenched her fists, bit her lip, and stood up. A moment later, the great sledge Harendar was in her hands, fire coursing over her knuckles and lighting up the hallway in bright reds and yellows.

I am NOT..." Harendar slammed into the wall, sending stone splinters everywhere. "...fucking DYING..." another slam, and shards hit her hands and face hard enough to break through her protective charms, "...in HERE!" A third, mighty blow brought the flagstone wall down, a mini-landslide piling rubble at Liara's feet to catch the droplets of blood which ran off her brow.

Gritting her teeth, she grabbed the rope and dragged Edison up, onto her back, keeping him off the sharp flagstone edges.

On she walked, returning the way they had come. Every step seemed to get harder and harder, and Liara's breath came in great, heaving gasps. The fatigue slowed her, wore her down, until she had to put Edison down onto the tunnel floor.

She knelt next to him and began checking, inspecting. *Is he hurt?* She examined him for injuries, looking at his face, his chest, his stomach...

She turned her face away, cheeks burning; that was what had been missing. Edison's clothing had become too big for him and fallen off as he ran.

At least she knew why he had been harder to carry – he was back to his normal self, and much heavier than she. A quick glance at her own hands and figure satisfied her that she had been restored as well.

Reaching again into her "toolbox," Liara pulled out a seafoam-green blanket, hand-woven – a masterwork – and laid it over Edison.

His even breathing was soothing, and Liara found herself drifting off, head against the hard stone wall. Her last thought before sleep claimed her was *I hope he isn't angry with me.*

As Liara slept, she dreamed.

In her dreams, she floated over the Earth, seeing its vastness, seeing the works of God and of Man – the forests, the highways, the globe, all of it seemed to spin almost impossibly fast, whirling in green and blue streaks, faster and faster.

Until it stopped.

Liara was looking at the land between Europe and Asia – the Middle East – at a small body of water which separated

(*Jordan and Israel*)

two nations.

For a few moments, nothing happened. The water moved back and forth in the hot desert wind, and Liara had time to think, *Where are all the fish?* before IT happened.

There was a *pulse,* a *wave,* which began in

the water and tore through it without moving it. As the wave left the water in an ever-expanding ring, Liara saw the plants and animals in its path wither and die, aging to corpses in moments and beginning to rot on the ground where they fell.

She could feel the wave weakening as it expanded outward; it was an explosion, not a thrust, and there was no additional force behind it. It was just a *shove* of power, of death, that devastated all life in its path, sparing none.

The wave grew, pressing toward the Israeli settlements of Ein Gedi and Neve Zohar. Liara flinched as the power rolled to the edges of these cities. People about to die, children and animals, flashed through her mind, thousands and thousands of lives about to be snuffed.

No!

Just as the deadly force was about to cross into the city borders, there was a low flash which drew Liara's attention, although no one else seemed to notice.

Liara saw, assembled at the city line, a ghostly battalion, a legion of figures she could only describe as Roman soldiers, shields locked together to face the threat.

The wave slammed into the interlocked shields, and Liara could see the dirt slide behind the legionnaires' boots as they dug in their heels.

The soldiers bent their heads and buckled behind their shields as the nigh-endless force pressed at them. An Israeli family was driving near the edge of the town, and the little boy was leaning out of the window, pointing and yelling.

The ranks of soldiers began to thin, troopers from the back moving forward to replace their fallen brethren. Liara felt a chill in her heart, but also felt the assault diminishing, the heat vanishing after an explosion.

Then it was gone. All of it. The child said one last thing to his parents, then retreated back inside his car.

Liara opened her eyes – it took her a moment to remember where she was

(*the Labyrinth*)

and why.

When her vision cleared, Liara saw Edison propped against the opposite wall, green blanket covering his lap. He was smiling.

<div align="center">~~~</div>

"Good morning. You've been out for a while – you been holding out on me?" He chuckled, and the chuckle turned into a full belly laugh as Liara narrowed her eyes at him. "The hard drugs, I mean." No recognition. "Valium, Percoset, those?"

"The...hard drugs? What...OH!" Realization hit her, and she began to laugh as well.

The laughter was long and hard, and it seemed to cast more light than did the strange and inexplicable radiance which came through the ceiling.

When the laughter subsided, Edison looked down at himself. "Do I need to turn this into a toga, then? Or do you have something in my size?"

Liara's grin was almost hurting her face at this point. "No, no need for a toga. I think I can manage something." Her smile disappeared, replaced by grim determination. "It's what I do, after all."

Liara sat on the cold stone and raised her hands. The rings and amulets she wore began to shine, radiating a kaleidoscope of colors that reflected off the tunnel walls like a disco hall in full swing.

Harendar, the great hammer, appeared, coruscating blue and gold flames wrapping around one of Liara's hands as she held the other out flat, resting it on an invisible anvil.

Liara never thought of what she did as "magic," as she knew some others did. Even when she was first invested with the Nature, she never believed in magic. What she did was impressive, yes...fantastical, perhaps...and so complex that the one Essential she had tried to explain it to had begged off.

But not magical.

Under the mighty blows of Harendar, Liara forged the very substance of the universe – matter, energy – into new forms. This was no act of magic, but of skill; each piece was inter-locked, tempered, and tested. This was an act of THE FORGE, and THE FORGE only created by breaking down weaker material and putting it through the crucible until it was pure.

At last, the work was done. Liara held a shimmering metal shirt, pants, underclothes and boots. The steel – if it could truly be called "steel" – was supple and smooth, more cloth than metal, and every scale held Liara's sigils of protection and strength within them.

Edison had watched this process with a look of intense interest. When Liara held out his new raiment – her eyes darting from his face to the clothes and back again – he took them, meeting her gaze.

"Thank you, Liara."

She smiled, a small, shy smile that broadened until it defined her face. It was beautiful.

"Turn around, please?" Liara hesitated, then nodded and averted her eyes. Edison smiled to himself as he dropped his makeshift kilt and slipped on Liara's gift.

The clothes felt like a soft breeze caressing his skin; he had to look down to make sure that he was actually wearing them. The touch was so light, it was easy to forget that they were there.

"It's okay now." He pulled the shirt over his head. Liara turned around, her eyes dancing over the garment, checking fit, hang lines, her face dropping into the analytical mask she reserved for evaluation of her own work.

"Is it all right?" Edison almost laughed at the painful and obvious earnestness in her eyes. "Any pinching, too heavy? It's tricky making metalcloth like this..."

"It's fantastic."

Liara relaxed, and Edison looked down at himself, stroking the shirt and pinching some of the material. "Is it as strong as I think it is?"

A wide smile appeared on Liara's face again as, without warning, she plunged a sharp knife toward Edison's heart.

His eyes were only beginning to register the attack before the blade struck home.

And shattered, the pieces flying like grenade shrapnel.

"Damn. Makes Frodo's mithril shirt look like tissue paper, doesn't it?"

Liara chuckled, then her face smoothed and she looked around. "We were getting younger as we went down this hallway." She pointed down the black expanse, which, even now, seemed to call, to beckon them.

"I know. I don't know how young I must have been when you caught me, but I was barely able to walk by then." Edison scratched his chin. "How did you figure it out? I know I didn't notice it."

Liara shrugged. "You were ahead of me, so I guess you were getting younger faster. Anyway, your voice sounded different, and then I noticed my hand had shrunk." Another smile. "It didn't take a rocket scientist to figure it out at that point."

"Well, I'm glad we didn't have a rocket scientist with us, then, or we might both be infantized." He cocked his head, smiling. "Infanted? Rendered infantile? What's the best term here?"

Liara ignored his comments. "Is she going to let us through, Edison? Or are we just trapped here?"

Edison considered the question, index fingers tapping together.

"I think we're close." His nostrils flared as he spoke. "The first thing that we – well, you – hit wasn't a serious problem. I know it was hard for you," he amended, raising his hands in defense, "but you weren't, *we* weren't in any real danger. This, however...this was a pretty hefty challenge – the kind that might have gotten us killed, you know?" Liara nodded. "I think that, maybe, if we can figure out a way past this tunnel, we'll get to see her."

Liara began to respond, but then she remembered something from her dream. A phalanx defending a City from Death. Two powers struggling against each other. Two Natures at war.

"Edison, I have an idea." Liara's voice quickened. "Her power is to make us lost, right? Makes this place hidden, makes it confusing, changes the paths. All things that can't happen in the, quote, 'real world,' right?" Edison nodded, but Liara was still speaking. "Your Nature lets you communicate with things – satellites, too, right?" A pause, a glance at his face for the affirmative. "Can you GPS us here?"

Edison laughed, then stopped as he saw Liara's face fall. "I'm sorry, but this place is off the grid. It doesn't exist, really. Not in any reality we know of." He held out his arms to encompass the whole of the Labyrinth. "It's her own private world."

"It HAS to exist, Edison, or we couldn't be here. Despoina's power is changing rules, altering laws." She looked him in the eyes. "If the place exists, it has to have a beginning and an end. You should be able to find it if it exists."

"Okay, granted, except I *can't*, Liara. It's not *here*. It's not *anywhere*."

"Dammit, Edison, YOU'RE here! You're

somewhere, aren't you? Reach out! Talk to those satellites, those networks! Communicate! Make them find you!" She grasped his shoulder. "Don't you see? If you can force the world, the universe, the multiverse, *whatever,* to acknowledge this place, then the place becomes subject to the laws of reality."

"Can that be done?" His eyes were wide, his breaths shallow.

"I don't know." She dropped her hand. "I know that Harendar has no weight in my toolbox until I pull him out, so it makes sense that other physical laws would apply. I was able to smash through her wall, even though she could have rerouted my path. I don't know." Her eyes were bright. "It's our only chance; we have to beat her at her own game, or else we'll be stuck here forever." She leaned in close to Edison's face, catching his restless eyes. "Will you try?"

Edison looked down, mind racing. Did she know what she was asking? They were in the very lair of an Essential – reality itself was twisted to serve Despoina's Nature. Edison wasn't even sure that this place *could* be reached, by anything, even by signals, without her permission.

He checked his cellphone. No reception. No surprise.

He flexed his will, a small piece, no real stress. *No sense in slamming myself against a brick wall.*

One bar. And a light twinge of pain behind his left eye.

Holy shit! Liara noticed the surprise on his face.

"What? What is it?"

He shook his head to clear it, then refocused on the phone. It had dropped back to zero reception.

Edison glanced over at Liara, then back to the phone. "I think we can do this." *Best not to think about possible consequences.*

He stole another glance. *Not while she's looking at me that way.*

"You can?" Her face was flushed. "What can I do? Anything?"

Edison shook his head. "You might have to help me walk. I might not be able to see where I'm going. And we'll need to move fast, too – I don't know how long

(*until I die*)

I can keep this up."

Liara's smile nearly wrapped around her entire face.

I wish she would be that happy saving my *life,* he thought before refocusing on his cellphone.

Find us, he said to it with all the strength he could muster. *Find us.*

An explosion of pain blossomed in his head, like an icepick had landed between his eyes.

The phone's touchscreen lit up like a city block after an explosion. Reception went to four bars, 4G active, finding your location...

Edison's mind – the part that wasn't doing the work, anyway – remembered the story of Sisyphus, condemned to Tartarus for his overweening pride and sentenced to forever roll a boulder uphill.

Rolling a boulder uphill forever would probably feel a lot like this.

The smartphone displayed a pulsing blue dot, and Edison's hopes soared as his nose started to ooze blood.

Route to center!

MAPPING 1289271 POSSIBLE ROUTES.

"Edison! Are you..." Liara began, but Edison waved her off.

250 FEET AHEAD, TURN RIGHT.

Okay. "Let's...go." He stumbled to his feet and started down the hallway

Each step was harder than the last, less and less of his concentration available to do anything except keep the lostness, the twisting of the paths, away – to keep this place *here*, where every road has a beginning and an end.

Right turn.

200 FEET, THEN CLIMB UPWARDS 50 FEET.

Step, step. The blood dripping from his nose resembled a leaky faucet more and more, and he was getting a stitch in his side as if he had been running. His head pulsed and swam like an overactive blowfish.

Step, step. On the wall. The sensation of vertigo knocked him off of his feet for a moment, but he stood again. Now he was panting, and blood hit his hand.

TURN LEFT, THEN TRAVEL 150 FEET.

Confusion

(*which way is left again*)

flashed through Edison's brain for a moment. His control slipped, the reception dropped to three bars. The phone spent two seconds

RECALCULATING

before restating: 150 FEET.

A brief nod, then quivering steps forward.

At 90 feet, the headache began piercing his eyeballs.

At 60 feet, he couldn't see anymore; he motioned with his left hand and, a few moments

(*an eternity!*)

later, Liara had him and was holding him up. He waved the phone in his right hand.

"Take...follow..." he managed, but could say no more.

30 feet. Edison's hands and feet were going numb. His tongue, too.

20 feet. He could feel the blood pounding in his brain, feel the vessels about to burst.

10 feet. He couldn't even hear or feel anything anymore. All that remained was the constant, overwhelming pressure, and the knowledge that he must...not...break.

YOU HAVE ARRIVED AT YOUR DESTINATION.

Edison did not have time to rejoice before

oblivion claimed him.

14 – LIAR IN THE STORY

Liara adjusted the wet cloth on Edison's forehead and checked his nose. It had stopped bleeding.

"I think he's all right." She sighed, turning toward her hostess.

Despoina clicked her tongue. "I did not think that anyone could pierce my veils." She poured the tea into delicate china cups at her stained cedar table.

Liara glanced back at the bed where Edison was lying. She smiled.

"He didn't really think he could do it, either." She put a gentle hand on his cheek. "But he never gave up."

Despoina's blue gown shimmered in the torchlight, a ghost in the windowpane as she moved Liara's cup of tea to her setting. Its color matched the walls, adorned by maps with glowing azure lines tracing impossible routes between impossible places. It was incomprehensible to Liara, but she had the feeling that, if she could understand what was written here, she could go anywhere.

Or everywhere.

"This is the first time that anyone has reached me without my express permission." Despoina took her seat in her mahogany throne, which was carved with vines, leaves, trees. "I have chosen to be pleased about this, rather than angry."

The smile disappeared from Liara's face. "Oh." She fumbled for the right apology. "We did not mean to bother you, but..."

"You had something of vital and urgent

importance? Something you need to find?" Despoina glared at her, and Liara shrank back from the blade in her gaze. "Of course you do. Everyone does." She waved her hands in the air, and Liara saw a strange gleam appear in her eye. "Oh, mistress, won't you help me? Find my treasure. Find my wife. Find my dog." Her voice had taken on a singsong rhythm as she continued. "Zippidee-doo-dah, where-oh-where has my little dog gone? The mistress can tell you, oh yes, tell you anything, lover's heart, lost courage, lost marbles! Anything...but is it worth it?" Despoina leered at Liara, looking her up and down. "Is it worth the mistress's while?"

"Wh...what is it you want?" The blood was draining from Liara's face. She's crazy. I'm trapped. What do I do?

Despoina cocked her head, smiling with her teeth, dark hair dangling, swaying. "It's not much, is it, dear, pretty, lovely? No, not much at all!" A hand

(a claw!)

reached out, and the fingers caressed Liara's face, nails against skin, almost scratching, but Liara did not dare flinch.

"There are many things that a woman like

you could give." Despoina's eyes roved over Liara's body, violating her. "Jewels, service...pleasures. Many, many pleasures."

Liara turned her face, unable to face the lascivious gaze leveled at her.

"But!" Despoina's spike in volume caused Liara to snap her head back. "I need none of these. Or, at least, none of them need me. No, no." She began swaying her head back and forth, to and fro, singing as she spoke.

"A memory, a memory, just one memory. A thought, a thought, I thought I thought a thought. One thought, two thoughts, enough thoughts to keep a thought of my own in! Ha ha ha!"

"...I don't understand." Liara tried to keep her voice from shaking.

"Simple! A memory, a thought, a piece of your mind to hold my own! An anchor, you see, against the madness!" Her eyes were blank, no one was home. "Lucidity, sanity, sense – just a taste – to hold back the creeping darkness from my own..." The smile vanished, and then she was back, her cheeks glistening with tears.

"Help me."

Liara leaned forward and took Despoina's

hands. "Are you all right?"

"No! More and more this happens…insanity, madness. I can no more defend myself against it than one can defend himself from the blood in his veins.

"My mind." She licked her lips, closed her eyes, reopened them. "It feels…burned, like a battlefield." Her gaze met Liara's. "I can find it for you, but you must meet my price. A bit of your sanity to bolster my own."

"But…" Liara hesitated.

"Please." She was begging. "Please."

A moment more, then, "The Egg exists? You can find it?"

An emphatic nod. "Yes! Will you pay? Will you?" Despoina's eyes never left Liara's, and neither did her hands.

"Yes." Liara closed her eyes and braced herself. "I will pay."

"Done!" Liara felt something…pulled…from her mind, leaving an empty

(not empty at all)

space where it had been. Despoina inhaled through her nose, then smiled again, but a more natural smile this time.

Liara opened her eyes. She felt all

right...she tilted her head, looking around the room for anything different, anything out of place.

Nothing except that strange emptiness, and even her awareness of that was fading.

"The Egg?"

Despoina's smile was wide as she reached toward a blank wall. Lines of golden light traced themselves into patterns, familiar land masses, continents, oceans.

A map.

"Just inside the border of the nation of Colombia." Glows highlighted the specified region as she spoke. "The Alabaster Egg lies within a river tributary, embedded in the water."

Liara stood and studied the map. "How can we find it?"

Despoina laughed. "Don't forget whose tea you have been drinking, my dear." Her hands waved, and the map expanded into a great doorway, red wood matching seamlessly with the wall.

Liara glanced over to where Edison lay. "Should we try to wake him?"

Despoina shook her head. "He strained himself terribly. Even the gods have their limits, little one. We should let him rest." She leaned over to look at Edison's face, and, for a moment, Liara thought she saw Despoina hunched, her dress moth-eaten and her body shriveled into little more than a skeleton.

Then it was gone.

Despoina walked to the doorway, and it opened as she approached, leading outward to a cascading river, pools of water, and animals playing among a verdant expanse of plants and life.

Liara stepped up to the opening, took one last look at the room, and Edison, then went through.

The door slammed shut behind her, making her jump.

Liara had entered the Amazon rainforest through the trunk of a great tree, some fifty yards from a large stream, which was heading north to join others.

Liara stepped through the foliage, confident that her amulets and rings would protect her from the incidental stings, scratches, or bites of the local flora and fauna. Mosquitoes avoided her, and thorns failed to find purchase in her skin or clothing.

A much more pleasant trip for me than for some others. The idea brought a smile to her face.

Liara arrived at the riverbank. The current was strong, and the water was tearing through its assigned path like a bulldozer, its attempts to cut a wider path opposed only by the thick greenery lining the banks.

An egg. Her brow creased. An egg.

"How the hell am I supposed to find an egg?!" She put her hands in her thick red hair. "How?"

"You're not." The calm, dangerous voice came from behind her. Liara spun around, Harendar appearing in a burst of fire in her hand.

Eriana sauntered out from behind a tree, eyes as dark as her dress. She advanced on Liara, holding the other woman's eyes with her own.

"Don't look so surprised, bitch." Eriana's smile was a knife-edge, glistening in the hot sun. "You're going to come with me. Azrael has something he wants to say to you."

The name still brought weakness to Liara's knees, but she tried her best to keep them steady. Eriana had stopped just outside the easy reach of her hammer.

"I'm not going anywhere." Liara leveled her hammer at Eriana. "You killed him, didn't you? Killed Oreth."

The cruel look on Eriana's face seemed to vanish like mist, and her eyes flicked to the left. "No, I didn't." She brought her eyes again to her adversary. "And what does it matter? Azrael wants you, and I intend to bring you."

"What if I say no?" Liara took a step back, raising Harendar overhead with both hands.

"Well, I am bringing you back." Eriana laughed, raising her hands in front of her chest. "If you think that toy can stop me, you just go right ahead." When Liara hesitated, Eriana thrust her chin out. "As they say, 'hit me with your best shot!'"

What is she doing? Liara glanced back and forth. It has to be some sort of trick.

"No?" Eriana leaned toward Liara, breathing into her face. "So you're a coward as well as a slut-bitch. Do you want to know what we did to your man, slut-bitch?"

"My...my man?" Liara's eyebrows went up and her hammer dropped a little. "He wasn't..."

"First I cut into his belly while he screamed. Not too deep at first – little, thin cuts just under the skin. His blood was hot on my hands." Her smile had become wicked, and Liara shook her head.

"Stop."

"Then I cut his fingernails out of their beds. That's not easy, you know – takes a special kind of tool to cut through there." The smile became even more predatory. "I didn't bother using the right tool.

"Before he died, he begged for us, for Azrael, to let him go, to let him die." A light was burning deep in Eriana's eyes as she spoke. "Oreth called your name, you know. 'Where are you, Liara? Help me! Save me!"

Eriana spat on the ground. "Feh. As if you could save him. You won't even take a swing at me when I'm standing here unarmed." She leaned into Liara's face. "Won't...even...fight...back."

Oh, Liara wanted to. The entire time Eriana had been speaking, taunting her, a red haze had begun creeping over her vision; anger had begun to confuse her thoughts and jumble her perceptions. Still, she held to her smith's discipline, focusing her mind, trying to block out the rage.

Eriana's eyebrows knitted together and she dropped her hands. "This doesn't make sense," Her eyes lowered. "You're supposed to lose control when I talk about him."

The strangeness of this statement shocked Liara back into normalcy. "What did you say?" she asked, as Eriana's eyes widened.

"Gods, you aren't in love with him anymore, are you?" She pointed at Liara's face, laughing. "It's that other one, that one you were with, isn't it? Maybe he should be the one strapped to my table..."

Liara could feel the mental snap; as she tried to block out Eriana's taunts she found there was no defense, no wall to put up. There was one moment of clear thought

(*You won't touch him*)

and then rage; fiery, hot, liquid metal in the mold, consumed Liara's being.

"SHUT UP!"

The hammer slamming into Eriana's face made a very satisfying schlock sound, caving in her cheek and knocking her into a massive tree, tearing up the roots and toppling it over. The next blow came from overhead, Liara bringing the sledge down on her enemy's chest, crushing ribs and puncturing lungs.

Tossing the hammer aside, Liara grabbed Eriana by the front of her dress, screaming "SHUT UP!" with each blow as she smashed her fists against the formerly beautiful face before her. Blood sprayed on Liara's knuckles, her arms, and her cheeks.

Liara lost track of the time she spent venting this rage and frustration

(why am I so angry?)

until she brought herself up. The world snapped back into focus, and Liara was standing over an unrecognizable corpse, covered in bits of blood, bone, and brain, clutching a torn dress in a death grip.

She dropped the mangled form of Eriana and ran, grabbing Harendar as she fled; she ran for several seconds, before remembering, Where can I go? I'm supposed to find the Egg.

(*Oreth's already dead why are you still here?*)

Doesn't matter. Find the Egg, figure it out later.

Tap, tap, on her shoulder. Liara froze for a

split-second, then turned her head.

Eriana stood behind her, smiling that evil, sadistic smile.

"We weren't done, bitch."

Liara felt the grip on her hammer weaken, the handle sliding halfway out of her hand.

"H...how?" Her knees were weak, and she couldn't stop her mind from racing.

"Lesson one." Eriana tapped Liara on the chest with a delicate finger – the force of impact hurled her through the air and crashing through trees like a stone fired from a catapult.

"Beating the shit out of me wasn't your mistake." She smiled, sauntering toward Liara as the other woman struggled to catch her breath and regain her feet. "It was why you were doing it."

Eriana tipped Liara's chin upward and looked in her eyes for a moment. She smiled at the wide-eyed fear

(*how is she so strong?*)

she saw within.

"You fought me because of what I had done, what I said I would do. You sought to harm me in payment for harm I had done." Eriana leaned forward. "There's a word for that, you know."

She whispered into Liara's ear one word: "Vengeance," and then followed it up with a backhanded slap that felt like a freight train. Liara was thrown to the ground, struggling to remain conscious, eyes on her left wrist.

The runes on the bracelet had shattered. Her protective wards were overcome.

Eriana hauled Liara back to her feet, clutching the woman's collar in her hands and grinning into Liara's swelling face.

"You stole my husband, you whore. I've waited a long, long time for this."

Liara managed to choke out a laugh. "You...you think I...stole Oreth from you?" Her body shook in Eriana's grasp. "He barely paid attention to me – he was always too busy being himself, serving his Nature. Even the time we spent together...he wasn't even there.

"He never loved me."

As the words left her lips, Liara realized that this was the first time she had been able to express this thought without feeling heartbroken, like something was wrong with her.

"He never loved me." She said it again, reveling in the freedom from the shame she once felt. "He left you because he wasn't capable of loving anyone anymore! It wasn't my fault!"

"Liar!" Eriana screamed, her spit flying in Liara's face. "You took him from me! You're the reason he ran away, the reason he abandoned me!" Eriana's eyes were wild as she shook Liara, who kept laughing.

"Sorry, *bitch*." Liara curled her lip at Eriana. "You've been pissed at me for centuries, thinking that I stole your man." She shook her head. "Think what you could have done with all that time you wasted." Liara smiled, her teeth stained red from her blood.

"SHUT UP!" Eriana's eyes glistened, tears welling as she swung a fist at Liara's laughing face.

Liara caught that fist with the ease of a father playing with a child.

"Here's my 'lesson one.' If you want to avenge something, the other person actually needs to have done something to wrong you." Liara's knuckles went white as she bore down on Eriana's closed fist. Her efforts were rewarded by the grating of crumbling bones and shrieks of pain from her foe.

Liara pushed Eriana's hand away from her,

sending the weakened Essential tumbling to the ground as Liara brought her hammer back up.

Eriana's eyes traced her doom's arc as it rose into the air. Fear was writ large across her face.

Her mouth moved, her voice a shadow in the air.

"No."

The hammerhead swayed in the air, flames flickering.

I should kill her now. Kill her

(*let her go*)

...What?

(*let her go*)

What the hell?

Eriana scrambled away as Liara's eyes narrowed and began to flit from side to side. When Liara refocused her vision, Eriana was gone. She lowered her hammer again.

Are you there? She drew her consciousness inward, searching for the source of the voice. *Is someone there?*

There was no answer.

Liara glanced around, taking in the massive trees, the canopy obscuring the sky, and the destruction the two Essentials had left in their wake.

"Damn. Where do I go now?"

The cell phone in her pocket rang. She blinked, pulled the phone out, looked, looked again as it kept ringing.

The caller ID said EDISON.

~~~

Edison woke up to see a cracking, decaying face, paper-thin flesh drawn over the bone, peering down at him, a thin smile on its peeling lips.

"Ah!" He screamed, backing away and sitting up.

"Hello, young man." The soft woman's voice was incongruous coming from the withered lips. "I didn't mean to startle you. Would you like some tea?"

Edison kept his head against the wall it was touching as he nodded, not trusting himself to speak. The dead woman walked toward the fireplace, her torn and unraveling blue dress dragging the ground.

I've heard that voice. Where?
~~~

"Your lady friend left about twenty minutes ago." The corpse-woman reached out to take the tea kettle. "I don't expect she shall return."

Edison inhaled sharply as realization struck.

"...Despoina?" He blinked. She was still there. "Wh...what happened to you?"

"What's that?" The zombie turned her dead eyes on Edison. "What do you mean?"

"Y...you're dead, Despoina."

The corpse nodded, dust creaking from her neck. Tears

(*how can a corpse cry?*)

welled up in her eyes, bringing the blue-grey once more to prominence.

"It is Azrael's doing." She took a seat near the crackling fire, her joints cracking and ten-dons straining. "Millennia ago, he came to me. One of his friends had vanished, and he needed my help. He had a deal for me, he said."

The threatened tears materialized, running down Despoina's mummified cheeks and dripping on the floor.

"He threatened me. He told me that he would kill me, painfully, for years, if I didn't agree. I knew that he could. When I looked in his eyes, I knew that he would.

"He wanted to link our Natures, to allow mine to express some of his. He said it would take some of the 'edge' off of him, so that he could move safely, without killing everyone and everything around him."

Despoina glanced at Edison, who nodded. There had been rumors of this, rumors that Azrael's power had grown beyond his own ability to control. Most Essentials believed that this was a deliberate ploy by Death, feigning weakness – or pretending strength! – where there was none, but this story spoke against that hypothesis.

"I did not wish to die. I did not. So I agreed. I let him turn the Pathways into Death's Roads, the crossroads, the ferryman, all reflections of that agreement, that deal.

"I couldn't know what that would do to me. Those I previously would have misled were killed instead. Paths twisted to deposit the lost into Azrael's hands. Worst of all, I became a vessel of Death...my body, slowly rotting away." She held out her hands, then looked down at her decrepit form.

Edison's mouth was agape as Despoina related her story. Then his eyes narrowed.

"Despoina...where is Liara?"

Despoina's tears grew heavier, and her voice began to hitch. "He...he sent a messenger. A beautiful woman with fiery eyes. She came just a short time before you – she told me to send Liara away, send her to the Amazon, and to take a particular piece of her mind, her sanity, as payment."

Edison's face was unreadable. "Which piece?"

"A piece of her willpower, something regarding her love." She spread her hands, then dropped them. "She would not be able to stand a threat to him, nor anything which might happen to him."

Edison stood, blood draining from his face. "You, you..." He sputtered, for once unable to come up with the right word. "You have to send me to her. Now!"

Despoina was shaking her head, and her tears quickened. "I can't. I won't. I don't want you to get killed too. I know that bastard Azrael is going to come for me once he doesn't need me anymore." Her face brightened, in a sense – the dead eyes now burned with an inner fire.

"Come with me, Edison." Her voice was seductive, but that voice coming from that face was...revolting.

"We can escape, hide together. I could be young again, find a way to separate myself from Azrael." Her eyes searched his, seeking any hint of acceptance, of hesitation. "Please?"

Edison put his hands up in a warding gesture. "Why would you help me? What's in it for you? Why risk pissing off Azrael?"

Despoina's gaze dropped to the ground. "Liara...I took a piece of her mind. Part of her is in me. It...she...wants you safe."

Edison advanced on Despoina.

"Listen to me." His words hissed from behind his teeth. "You're afraid of him, of Death...but you've become death! Look at yourself!" Edison gestured towards Despoina's rotting, cadaverous form.

"You can't outrun Azrael. It never works — never has. Think of Alemandreus. Think of Glorianna. But you can stand up to him. Refuse to be afraid. Refuse to be corrupted." A laugh. "All he can do, really, is kill us. Our Natures live on, even if we don't, even if we die. He can't touch those without our help."

Despoina's tear-filled eyes were fixed to Edison's face as he spoke. "Why are you saying these things?"

"Because someone showed me that there's more to being one of us than living forever. Immortality is just a side benefit, Despoina." Edison pulled out his cellphone, waved it at her as he spoke.

"I can see the waves, the information, transmitted all over the world. I can tap into the Internet, bypass passwords, read any language and speak to anyone anywhere. This is more than I ever dreamed of in my mortal days, when I was just a man who loved his country so much that he left his family behind to serve it, that he ran for days to save it."

He barked a harsh laugh. "I've experienced so much that I could never have imagined. Shouldn't that be enough? Do I need to live forever? I've lived over two thousand years." His voice was rising with his blood. "I've loved every one of them! Who cares if I die now? Two thousand years, Despoina. Longer for you, I know. Hasn't it been long enough?" He took her hands. "Aren't some things worth dying for?"

Despoina's face was averted, unable to meet Edison's eyes. Her tears pattered on the floor, but she made no attempt to wipe them from her rotted cheeks.

"Help me help her, Despoina. Fuck Azrael, (*damn that felt good!*)

fuck dying – do something. Stand up for the Ways, for your Nature – don't let your soul die because you're afraid to let your body go. Stand up for who you really are."

Seconds passed. The two were frozen, a still-frame taken from a movie. The only evidence of time's passage was the in-and-out of breath.

Despoina's head began to shake back and forth. "I can't." Her voice cracked as she repeated it, once again peering into Edison's eyes, but this time for forgiveness or understanding. "I can't."

Edison's face smoothed out, the passion floating away. "Fine." He turned away from his corpselike hostess and glanced around. "Where's the damn door? I'll save her myself then."

Despoina's head snapped up. "No! You can't go! He'll kill you! He'll destroy you!"

Edison's lip rose in a snarl. "Maybe he will, but at least I'll die trying to protect something I care about. At least I'll be trying, goddammit. More than you can say."

"I won't let you. I won't let you leave. He can't hurt you if you stay." She came up behind him. "He can't get to us in here if I don't let him."

"I got through once before, you know." Edison moved away, feeling the walls with his hands as he spoke. "I'll do it again, even if it kills me."

"You would do that? Risk your own life, twice over, rather than leave her behind?"

Edison stepped back from the wall, appraising it, still not looking at Despoina. "In a heartbeat."

"...there's nothing? Nothing I can do? No gifts I can grant you to keep you here? No words that will convince you?"

Edison turned, his eyebrows raised. "No. Nothing. I'm leaving."

Despoina sighed, then nodded. "If you go, then you have my blessing, and the blessing of the Ways." Edison was about to speak, but Despoina went on. "The true Ways."

"What are you talking about..." Edison began, then his breath caught as he watched her.

Despoina had raised her hand to her eyes, watching in marvel as the skin and flesh – what was left of them, anyway – flaked away like ashes on the wind.

"It's no wonder." She turned her eyes toward Edison for a moment before resuming her vigil over her body's dissolution.

"What, Despoina?" His voice was reverent as he watched the death of a god, the passing of a guardian.

She shook her head and giggled. "Sorry, not for me to say, really." Her eyes smiled in her corpse face. "Can you promise me something, my dear?"

Edison nodded. "I can try."

The decay had accelerated – Despoina's face had begun to fall apart, small pieces of her forehead and chin spinning off into the air.

"Ensure that the next holder of my Nature does not fall as I did. Help them learn and to do it justice." Her eyes were the only flesh left on her head.

"I will."

Despoina's eyes rolled back, and she crumbled in on herself, a boneslide that left only a light dusting on her chair and dress.

Well, that was anticlimactic. Edison allowed himself a smile.

Then the nuclear bomb hit.

The force emanating from the place of Despoina's death threw him against the wall. It left him shielding his eyes against its radiance and praying that the screaming sound would end.

For just a moment, Edison sat at the center crossroads, linked to every path, avenue, and byway – he knew the passageways between now and then, here and there and everywhere.

Then it was gone, and he was just here, himself again, sweating and overwhelmed. He picked himself up off the floor, shaking the dust out of his hair, staring wide-eyed at the site of the explosion of power.

The power had left a scorch mark, black with veins of red, on the ceiling as it left.

Edison looked more closely. *Those red lines...they weren't just random...what?*

Africa. Libya. X marks the spot. He glanced at his phone. Cracked, but still working. 4 bars.

"Call Liara."

Ring...ring...

"Edison?"

"Yeah. You're on the wrong continent, darling."

"What? What do you mean?"

"Get to the nearest airport – I'll meet you there. We're going to Libya."

Edison hung up the phone before Liara could reply, and looked out a window. Instead of an other-worldly landscape, however, it now showed a very confused crowd of Greek tourists and a more confused group of American bus riders.

"Where's a neuralyzer when you need one?"

~~~

"So she just...let herself die?" Liara's voice was low, mindful of the passengers surrounding them. Edison had briefed her on what had happened in Despoina's room while she had been gone.

Edison nodded, his face drawn and thoughtful. "Yeah...and remember how I said
~~~

that I touched her Nature for just a moment? I didn't feel any Death in it at all – I think she must have taken it all into herself, died to keep the Ways pure."

Liara looked out the plane window at the Iquitos airport. Edison had taken her rapid appearance in stride – after all, it had only taken him about seven hours to get here – but Liara had actually been waiting for quite a while.

About six hours and forty-five minutes, in fact.

What Liara hadn't told him was that, after hanging up the phone, she had known how to get to Lonato. Even after re-forging her wards, it would have taken her several days to get there...so she had just willed it.

And it had worked. Just like when Oreth did it

(*used to do it*).

Even here, in the city itself, Liara felt a sense of comfort, as if she were in the embrace of a dear grandmother, with warm kitchen smells tickling her nose and throat.

"Liara?"

Edison's voice brought her out of her fugue. She smiled at him. "Sorry, Edison. I was just thinking."

"About what?"

"Who would have thought that these last few days would be like this?" He nodded as she spoke. "I mean, first we find Oreth again, then all hell breaks loose. I don't remember the last time I felt like I was actually in danger, afraid for my life, my wellbeing."

Edison pursed his lips, looked down, then looked back at Liara. "Hey, how did you find him, anyway? I didn't feel him until he woke up, got part of his memory back. He'd been missing for a really long time...how long?"

Liara's smile touched the corners of her mouth. "The fall of Rome against the Visigoths in the 5th century." Her eyes drifted off into the mists of the past. "He fell in battle, defending his Nature, defending the Eternal City against the attackers." Memories and emotions were flooding her now, some clear, others

"Great Gods, I'm dying. Help me." His prayer seemed unheeded by anyone, and he fell as he watched the approach of the white-robed figure walking across the battlefield toward him, as he felt the cold hand on his heart.

fogged, hidden.

Edison blinked. "Were you there? What could have killed him?"

Liara shook her head. "I don't know. Whatever it was laid waste to half of both armies before it left; I thought he was dead.

"What was left of Rome's legions met the enemy, but the battle went against them. Historians say it was lead poisoning." They both laughed a little.

"I remember his face." She lost focus once more, seeing the ancient scene more clearly than the airplane. "He was so scared. He was dressed as they were, but in arms I had forged for him, and still he was scared.

"I told him not to go, to let the soldiers fight, to use his powers if he had to but not to take the field himself because he could be killed. He looked at me, and he was so pale, Edison, so bloodless, and he said, 'I can't, Liara. Rome is marching. Rome needs defending. Gods help me if I go, but Rome needs me.'"

"He really said that?" Edison frowned. "I had never seen him risk his life before."

"Neither had I, but Rome was special to him. He used to call it the 'center of the universe' because all roads supposedly led to

Rome." Edison nodded.

"The one thing he cared more about than his own life was his Nature." A single tear wound its way down her cheek and ran off her chin. "It's why mankind had such success settling, colonizing, building cities. He lived it, breathed it, believed in it. Nearly died for it." Liara's breath began to hitch.

"Liara, it's okay, I can ask him when we save him, you don't need to..."

Liara burst into sobs. "No, you can't, because he's dead! They killed him, Edison, killed him, pulled his skin off and tortured him to death!"

Edison pulled back, and others on the plane looked confused at the sudden outburst; many of their fellow passengers did a good job of acting deliberately deaf.

"And now, somehow, his Nature came to me!" Tears were rolling now, reddening her eyes. "I keep hearing and feeling things that I'm not used to and that I haven't heard before – and there's something behind them, like someone watching and whispering."

Edison's mouth worked, but he made no sound. Liara took no notice. "And now they're after me...we couldn't save him and he's going to come for me now and do the same thing they did to Oreth!" Words failed her and she just sat in the chair, crying into her hands as the plane moved closer to their destination in Tripoli.

Edison was still for a few minutes as the fear and sorrow ran out of her eyes and through her fingers, then reached up and took her hands away from her face. Her teary eyes danced around, looking at him, then away.

"Listen to me, Liara. This is not your fault. Oreth did not die blaming you."

"How can you know that?"

"He sent you his Nature." Edison paused, letting that sink in. "He didn't send it to me, or send it away, or let it find another...he sent it to you."

Liara opened her mouth, closed it again. Glanced down. Glanced back.

"Before we left, when we came to save you, Azrael showed us something. He...he had your life, Liara, your essence, in a ball in his hands. I remember how Oreth's face looked when he saw that – he was scared, but not for himself. He was scared for you." Edison nodded to himself, remembering. "If he was able to send you his Nature, I bet that he also found a way to get your life away from Azrael."

Liara's eyes had gone wide as Edison had described the situation in which they had found her, but now they went blank as her focus turned inward. Her consciousness passed through the layers of her soul, seeking that spark, the very life itself she had been born with and which was wedded to her Nature.

It was there, blazing blue-white fire, hotter than any star in the sky...but something else was there with it, like an embryo curled in on the flame of her life, living off its warmth, pulsing. Its shell was a translucent white, and there was something inside, but what it was Liara could not tell.

Liara came back to herself. Edison was waiting for her. "Well?"

"No...my life...it's here, Edison, still here. But something else is there too..." Liara hesitated. It was hard to explain...the thing

(*life*)

had felt familiar but...could it really be?

(*yes*)

"I...I think Oreth sent his life along with his Nature!" Her eyes shimmered, a mix of joy and pain.

"What?!" Edison sat upright. "Is...is that even possible? Can we do that?"

She shook her head, laughing. "That's whose voice I've been hearing, Edison! He's not dead, not really...it's...it's like..." She paused, groping for the words, "...like a seed, almost like he's asleep, mostly dreaming..." She shook her head again. "I don't know how, but it's true. It's true." Liara's eyes sought Edison's, searching his face for approval or the lack thereof.

"Damn." A patch of turbulence forced Edison to pause and hold his coffee cup in place as the "Fasten Seatbelt" sign lit up again. "Not only did he keep Azrael from getting what he wanted...whatever that is...he managed to swipe your life-force out from under his nose and actually get it back to you – and smuggle himself in the process! That's just...damn." He sat back, shaking his head and laughing.

"Edison." Her voice drew his gaze up to look back at her. "Can we save him? Can this Alabaster Egg save him? If it is what we think it is?"

Edison bit back one of his trademark "who knows?" remarks, and said, "I hope so, but we have to be prepared in case it doesn't. We're on new ground, you know..." He couldn't hold the smile back any more. He gave Liara a sidelong glance and asked, "Isn't it exciting? Just a bit?"

Liara just stared at him for a second, unsure whether she was about to scream or cry. Instead, she laughed and nodded. "Maybe. Also terrifying, heartbreaking, and earth-shattering."

"Still exciting, though?"

"Yes, Edison. Still exciting."

Liara locked eyes with Edison and licked her lips, preparing to speak...but the emergency lights went on.

"Passengers, please be seated. We have a situation in the cockpit, and we need to make a..." The voice on the intercom shrieked, the sound piercing eardrums as it turned into a disgusting, gurgling death-rattle.

Edison's face lost all its amusement. "Oh, no."

The passengers began to scream like injured rabbits, panic setting in. Fights broke out in the aisles – an older man was thrown to the floor in the chaos and trampled underfoot.

A little Colombian boy traveling with his

grandfather started to yell.

"Papa! Papa! Los demonios! Los –" and then he was silenced as his young heart exploded from within.

Liara could feel the power twisting around them, seeking them; it was unable to penetrate all of these souls. There were too many lives in the way, so the power was removing them first.

A mother and her infant were pressed against a window, the both of them wailing, begging for mercy from whatever unholy force this was.

Edison unbuckled his seatbelt and pushed his way to them, wrapping them in his arms. He nodded over his shoulder at Liara.

Liara unsheathed Harendar, its flames going unnoticed in the panic.

If he's looking for us, I'll throw a little dirt in his eye.

She hurled the hammer at the plane's engine, through the wall. Oxygen masks fell as the pressure plummeted, but the fear of decompression only lasted a few seconds.

The explosion that shattered the wing commanded everyone's attention shortly thereafter.

The fire raged through the cabin, incinerating, burning, threatening to devour everyone and everything in its path. Liara saw the flames cascade over Edison and his two wards, heard the infant scream.

She raised her hand, palm to the flame as it raced toward her.

<<Bank, Flame. The Fire of the Forge you are, and I command you. Burn metal, not flesh. Feast on steel and be satisfied.>>

The fire shrieked as its appetite was diverted, and the plane shed screaming pieces of itself as its other wing splintered and sent the craft into a complete free-fall.

The blue-grey of the ocean caught them.

INTERLUDE

Azrael withdrew his consciousness from the airplane, his brows closing together. He rubbed his temples with his fingers.

"Is there trouble...Azrael?" Eriana kept her distance, standing near the entrance of the room and staying out of range of his aura, which seemed to have increased in strength over the last day or so, reaching out much farther than before.

Azrael glanced back at her from his meditation seat in the middle of the barren stone chamber, then stood.

"I almost had them, and then...something forced me out. Fire, I think – one of the humans probably started the plane burning in their panic. I couldn't maintain my presence there." He exhaled through his nose.

"Are they still alive?"

He looked at Eriana. "Are you a fool, woman? These are Essentials – a plane crash won't kill them." He clenched his teeth as he spoke. "They were there, I could feel their presence, but I hadn't pinpointed them.

"It's best this way – we know where the plane went down, the woman still has the Nature and, if we're fortunate, their efforts to survive have fatigued them." He took a deep breath. "Still, we must not allow them to reach Tripoli. Once in the city, they will be nearly impossible to find."

Azrael's eyes cut into Eriana's. "You must act before they reach land. Once they do, the woman may be able to transport them directly to the city, as Oreth could. Do you think you can round her up this time?" He smiled a cruel, mocking smile. "Preferably *without* hitting her hammer with your face?"

Eriana hissed, but his eyes held her.

"Of course."

"Get there, then." He turned away from her. "They crashed off the western African coastline. They will be heading toward the shore, looking to find shelter and civilization. Stop them before they do."

15 – VENGEANT VENGEANCE

"You never did tell me how you found Oreth." Edison was rowing with one of the makeshift oars Liara had constructed; she had tried her best to seem relatively "normal" so as not to further panic the crowd, and so had refrained from using her power to simply forge something akin to a luxury cruise-liner. The raft she had made, however, still stretched the boundaries of credibility just a bit. "Had you been looking for him long?"

Liara nodded, putting the final touches on the sun-shade she had built for the civilians. Most were shaken, but the worry was lifting now that Liara had been able to craft a workable barge for them to use to get to land.

"Yes." She put up a hand to shade her face, looking for land. "Oh, there were times when I thought I felt him, or felt his power flare. I always went immediately if I could, but I never found him. A few hundred years ago, I crossed Azrael's trail after he had gone, and realized that Azrael was looking for him as well." She considered, eyes looking to the left. "I think he was trying to hide from us."

"You think the amnesia was an act?"

Liara paused, pursed her lips, then shook her head. "No. I can't be sure, of course, but if what you were telling me is true, then he's too different, now, for him to have been faking. Don't you agree?"

Edison laughed. "Definitely." He stopped for a moment, stretching in his seat. "I still remember how surprised I was when he asked me to come with him to save you. That was something I had never expected to hear Oreth say in a thousand years." He looked Liara full in the face. "I'm glad he did, though."

Liara's skin flushed red, and she glanced down. Her eyes skittered, landing on several different places but refusing to settle. Finally, she whispered, "Me, too."

Edison reached out and took Liara's hand, bringing it to his lips. "To be continued." He flashed a wicked smile. "See, I caught wind of what was going on through the grapevine, as it were." Liara arched an eyebrow.

"Grapevine?"

Edison chuckled. "When you hear about a hospital room imploding on itself, it piques the curiosity. I checked the CC cameras and there you two were." He paused, glancing up and down Liara's body. "Although, what you were doing in a Playboy nurse's costume I would love to know."

Liara laughed, a deep belly-laugh that almost made her lose her grip on the rope she was holding. Her eyes watered, and Edison moved forward to take the rope.

"That damn outfit!" Tears were still rolling

down her face. "I didn't have time to make one myself; I was worried that he might vanish again, or that Azrael would get there before I did, so I had to...'acquire' one. Damn thing was two sizes too small – I felt like I was going to split it or fall out of it!" She laughed again.

"Just imagine how it must have looked to him." Edison put his hands up as if framing a picture. "Red-haired hooker-nurse straight out of a porno telling him he needed to run off with her." Liara gaped for a moment, then they both laughed again.

"I don't know what was going on with him while he was unconscious, but whatever methods he was using to hide himself had broken down – it was like I could see him through a shattered one-way mirror, you know?" She flicked over to Edison's face; he nodded, she continued. "When I sensed his presence, I just hopped in my mech and jetted over." Her brow crinkled, "And Azrael destroyed my damn mech in New York." She sighed.

"And the fight?"

Liara handed him the rope. "Pull this." She watched as Edison hoisted the sail onto the new mast. She checked over the rigging, looking for imperfections.

Liara grunted. "All right." She nodded her head, then looked back at Edison. "The fight? Your cameras didn't catch that?"

"The emergency power only lasts so long...and you can't catch Azrael on camera unless he wants to be seen."

"Right, I'd forgotten about that." Liara tapped her chin, thinking. Then she shrugged and smiled. "Not much to tell, really. I swung Harendar at Azrael's face, and Oreth vanished."

Edison's eyes were wide. "You...actually *swung* at Azrael?" He blinked several times. "What happened?"

"Oh, he went flying – laws of physics and all that. He crashed right into an EKG unit, actually. Didn't seem to bother him much. He just got up, bleeding a little, I guess, then he pointed, and my mech just kind of...fell apart, and down I went." Another shrug. "The rest you know."

"Damn." Edison's smile threatened to stretch off of his face. "I don't think anyone has ever swung at him...not as long as I've been alive, anyway." He gazed at Liara with renewed respect.

"Look!" Liara stood and pointed. "Land!" She tugged at the rigging and aimed their craft toward the coastline, just visible on the horizon.

The civilians started to cheer, clapping each other on the back and dancing in place. Some cried with relief, others with grief, and some just sat in the shade and thought about the story they would be able to tell their fellows back home.

Edison felt a tap on his shoulder.

<<Sir?>> It was the young woman with her infant, the one Edison had shielded from the fire, though the intensity of the flames had broken the ward-sigils Liara had placed on his armor. <<Thank you for saving our family.>>

Edison smiled. <<I was honored to be of service to you, Madam.>>

The woman's glance fell on Liara, then flicked back over to Edison. <<I do not understand what has happened here today.>> She moved her hand in the Sign of the Cross. <<But it is clear that God sent you to deliver us from evil...and you have.>>

The woman unclasped a necklace and pressed it into Edison's palm. Attached to the chain was a small figure crafted from gold.

<<Saint Michael.>> She released the figure and took a step back. <<He wards off evil. He helped you save us, and I want him to protect you now.>>

Edison took the gift, smiled, and clasped it around his neck. The mother returned his smile and retreated back to where another passenger was caring for her daughter.

Liara had a soft smile touching only the corners of her mouth as Edison sat back down. She sat next to him. "How does it feel to be someone's hero?"

"I should be asking you. Remember that old guy on the bus?" A short pause. "What are we going to do when we hit land?"

"I actually wanted to ask you about that. I don't think that Azrael has given up on us just because our plane exploded, do you?"

Edison shook his head. "As soon as he knows where we are, he'll come after us again. Maybe even kill us this time. We need to be ready."

"Do you think he'll send Eriana again?"

"Yeah, I do. I don't think Azrael is ready to show himself just yet, especially now that Despoina has died and unlinked their Natures." Another grin split his face. "In fact, I imagine that has probably pissed him off royally."

"Oh, hell. What if you're right? What if Azrael just can't control his power anymore? What if he totally loses his grip on it? What..." Her eyes were wide and her voice frantic. "What if he just let it go?"

"Shhh, shhh." Edison brought a finger to his lips. "One thing at a time. First, we worry about getting these people to safety, then we find that damn Egg."

Liara nodded. "All right, How are we going to get this many people through the plains? I know you can't call for help or else Azrael might be able to find us."

Edison checked his phone, which had survived the smoke damage and water from its recent travails. "Well, it looks like we're landing here..." He pointed on his map. "The nearest city is...Rabat, it looks like, in Morocco. We can get from there to Tripoli, right?"

Liara glanced down as she nodded. *Could I have just brought us all there?* she wondered. *Why haven't I tried? Is it to avoid being found...or because I'm afraid?*

"How far to Rabat from the coast?"

"Not far. About four or five miles."

A chill ran up Liara's back, causing goose-bumps to ripple down. She searched inward, asking the Other

(*Oreth*)

within her if there was something wrong, but the feeling she got in reply

(*run run hide*)

made little sense to her.

But it was there.

"Edison." Her eyes continued scanning the coastline. "I think that something's waiting for us over there."

Edison's right eyebrow rose. "What do you mean?"

"I...I think Oreth," and here she put her hand on her chest without realizing it, "I think he knows something, he can feel something over there." She put her hand down, and her face was set. "We need to be off this boat."

Edison glanced at the coastline, then nodded. "Okay. We can swim, I guess. Come ashore somewhere else. Just get a little wet, get a little wild."

"All right." Liara started rolling up her

sleeves and stowing her tools in the Otherspace. "Let's get going."

As she prepared to jump, she felt a presence behind her. She brought herself up short and turned to see.

A plump, elderly gentleman in a tweed jacket and tie, looking a bit worse for wear, was standing beside her, his head down.

She leaned toward him. <<Can I help you?>>

The man's face snapped up, and Liara saw a fierce gleam, almost a flame, in his eyes. His lips were curled in a snarl and his teeth were bared like a rabid dog's.

<<It's your fault!>> His scream was the sound of tearing metal, and he swung his fist at Liara's head. The blow struck home, stinging her cheek and causing her eyes to widen.

She turned back to her attacker, raising her arm to ward off more blows. *That shouldn't have hurt.*

<<What are you doing?>>

<<Mommy, what's going on? Where are you going?>> cried a little boy. A quick glance revealed the cause of his dismay; every adult had risen and was shambling, zombie-like, to-

ward the end of the barge that held the two Essentials. Their faces were twisted, angry, and the passengers hurled both recriminations and pieces of the barge at Liara and Edison.

<<You did this to us!>>

<<We're going to die, and it's because of you!>>

<<Why'd you have to get on our plane, fuckers?!>>

"What the hell is going on?" Edison ducked to dodge the detritus flying through the air. "What's gotten into them?"

The crowd had swarmed Liara, and she was struggling to keep their clawing and biting away, struggling to protect herself without hurting anyone.

"Something, that's for sure!" A pocketknife tangled in her clothes. "My wards aren't stopping...aagh!" Teeth sunk into her hand, leaving a crimson crescent moon gleaming on her skin. The punches and kicks increased in ferocity, as if the shedding of blood had triggered a feeding frenzy.

<<Got somethin' for ya, bitch!>>

<<How do *you* like it, huh?>>

<<That's what you get! Suck on it!>>

Edison was on his feet, trying to pull rage-zombies off of Liara, to free her from the press of flesh she was trapped beneath. One woman turned on him, slashing across his face and laying it open with a diamond on her finger. Edison fell, clutching at his wound.

"They're too strong!" He touched his face, confirming his injury before regrouping. "Liara!" He dived in again, fighting to reach her.

Liara was curled up, clothes ripping as her attackers fought, kicked, bit, tore at her. Red rivulets poured from several minor cuts, running down onto the deck.

Edison managed to pull one, a teenaged boy almost foaming at the mouth, off of the pile and throw him into the sea. The boy began treading water.

<<Fucker threw me in the fucking water! Get that son of a bitch!>>

Without hesitation, the crowd turned on Edison, charging and overbearing him, knocking him down.

Liara took a moment to gather her wits; when reality caught up to her, she realized that Edison was now the one in danger. Harendar appeared in her hand, responding to her desire to sweep them away, to clear the deck of these monsters that were once people, to free Edison from the mad crowd intent on his life.

As Edison squirmed beneath the passengers, the Saint Michael medallion that the woman had given him a short while ago fell out of his shirt. Instantly the attackers recoiled, shrieking obscenities and falling back.

What is going on? What's wrong with them?

Liara called to him. "Edison! The medallion! It's driving them off!"

Edison tore the medallion's chain and held it high; the rage-filled passengers hissed and clawed at the invisible barrier, but were unable to come near the two Essentials. He edged closer to Liara, making sure to keep the medallion visible.

"What the hell just happened?"

"I'll explain in a minute. Hold on tight." Liara reached out a hand to her companion. He took it.

She closed her eyes, concentrating. *I hope I know what I'm doing.*

For a moment, there was nothing; then, like a voice echoing from the distant walls of a canyon, *TRIPOLI* beckoned back.

The two Essentials vanished, leaving behind a crowd of confused onlookers whose anger dissipated as soon as the targets of it were gone.

A crowd of confused onlookers about to run aground.

INTERLUDE

Eriana looked upon the mortals disembarking from their barge; she could see the marks made by Liara's accursed hammer as it bent fuselage and hull into shape as only the Forge could do.

She had failed again. Somehow, the two had managed to halt the vengeful power aimed at their craft and escape.

She wields his power well. She looked down, then rubbed her hands over her eyes.

I...we...didn't think that she could harness it to travel such a distance.

Some of the survivors were checking their phones, hoping for a signal. Others were talking about how the two people who had saved them from drowning had vanished into thin air. Eriana closed her eyes and leaned against a tree, crumpling.

I can't go back. He'll kill me if I go back. I have to stop them or he'll murder me where I stand.

Perhaps two Essentials were too much for even her power. *Perhaps I need to divide them somehow. Break them apart, and conquer them individually.*

Eriana laughed as she invoked the *Erithkul*, the Spell of Moving that Azrael had taught her. She would follow them, arrange events to separate them, and then she would have victory...and vengeance.

(*For what?*)

Eriana's smile faded. If the bitch

(*Liara*)

had been telling the truth, then there was nothing for her to avenge, no wrong that they had done to her that she could seek retribution for. Her defeat at Liara's hands had certainly indicated that she may have been truthful; all they had done, then, was try to bring Oreth back, to save him.

Oreth's life belonged to her. He needed to be punished for what he had done. But he was dead.

As she vanished, leaving behind a small ring of charred grass, she wondered, *What if they somehow save him? Would that change anything?*

16- RAGGED AT THE CORNER

Liara and Edison stumbled out of a women's public restroom, causing civilians to point, scream, and cover their children's eyes.

Liara glanced at herself and Edison; once again, the two of them were in dire need of replacement clothing – Liara's utility outfit was shredded and Edison's metalcloth dented and cut open in several places.

Edison's eyes fell on Liara's torn apparel and scratched skin.

He suppressed a laugh.

"What's so funny?" Liara's hands were on her hips and her eyebrow arched.

"You...you look like," laugh, "you lost a fight," held in laugh, "with a pack of wombats!" Loud, whooping laughter.

"...Wombats? Really?" Liara shook her head, but the corners of her mouth were twitching. "Let's get some clothes, wombat-boy." She turned, trying to keep her figure as concealed as possible from the curious Libyans who were passing by. "I'm fresh out, you know."

"Can't make any more?

"Really? I should fire up the Forge in the middle of downtown Tripoli? That's a fabulous way to stay hidden, don't you think?"

Edison spread his hands. "I've got it, no problem." He headed toward a clothing store with a wooden sign in Arabic script: Al-Mulabis.

"And hurry!"

Edison stepped into the shop. The air was muggy, hot, smelling of fabrics and plastics.

The fluorescents changed the colors just a bit, causing Edison to blink as he entered.

The shopkeeper, a young man of about thirty or so, was picking at his mustache when Edison came up to the counter.

"Can I help you, man?" The cashier's English was passable, but his accent was heavy.

<<I need clothes, sturdy ones, for my wife and me.>> Edison slipped into a smooth Arabic, extending a handshake to the other man.

<<Well, I'm not sure if I have anything like that. Maybe you can come back tomorrow.>> The clerk continued picking at his mustache, glancing to Edison now and again.

Edison reached through his pocket, into his own Otherspace, and pulled out a ten-dinar note. <<I would really appreciate it if you could check the back for us.>>

The note disappeared and the cashier was off, hunting through shelves and crates.

<<Sturdy, you say? We have good leather, very strong. Also some military surplus, boots, pants.>> He brought up several different articles, including some traditional Muslim women's clothing, complete with headdress.

<<I don't think she'll want those, my

friend,>> Edison laughed to himself. <<I'll take the rest, though.>>

The cashier scribbled on a yellow pad, glancing through the clothes and jotting down numbers.

<<Three hundred and five.>> Edison nodded, handing him seven 50-dinar bills.

<<Keep the change. Peace be upon you.>>

<<And upon you.>>

Edison walked out the door of the shop and glanced around, looking through the crowds...but he did not see Liara.

"Liara? Liara? Where are you?"

Several women were passing by in full coverings, grey, green, black; some children were kicking a ball in the road. A white-robed form shuffled toward the store.

"Liara!" Edison's voice rose in volume, panic creeping in. Where was she? Did Eriana or Azrael come for her while he was gone? Had she just left, or...

"Right here."

His head whipped around, seeking out the source of that whisper. "Where? I can't see you."

The woman in the white hajaab and body-covering looked into Edison's face with her forest-green eyes. He leaned in.

"Liara? What happened to you?"

Liara smiled. "Some very nice ladies saw me, and decided that it would be cruel to allow my continued exposure to the lustful gazes of men, so they gave me this."

"They really said that?"

Liara tilted her head. "Not *exactly*, but that was the idea. One of them said something else interesting, though."

"What was that?"

"Apparently, the Berber tribes have said that they found new water in the desert. They are claiming that Allah touched the Earth to bless the Arabic people, and that this is a sign of a new age."

"So?"

She sighed. "*New* water? Water with grass and trees, water that cures wounds as well as quenches thirst?"

Edison stared. "Why didn't you say so?" Then he frowned. "Wait, if the Egg has been there..."

"Why is the water just now there? Who knows. Maybe it takes a while. Maybe it wasn't always there. I don't know, Edison, but I can feel it. That's where it is."

Edison nodded. "All right," he said, "we'll try it." He handed Liara the bundle of clothing and took out a few items for himself. "Here, if you want any of these – I'm going to go change."

Edison put on the old military gear, erring on the side of durability. *After all, who knows what'll be there when we arrive?*

When he came out, Liara was still in the white hajaab. He raised an eyebrow, and she shrugged.

"I'm less conspicuous this way."

"Fair enough." Edison began walking, and Liara moved up beside him. "By the way, you promised to explain why this amulet held off the rage-monsters." He held up the medallion of Saint Michael.

"Oh, that." She laughed. "It's simple. The medallion was given to you as a sign of gratitude for what you had done, right?"

"...Yeah..."

"See, gratitude is a counter to vengeance; one appreciates what you have done while the other seeks revenge. Two forces in opposite directions. Because someone was grateful to you for the same thing that the others were angry at you for, the true, real gratitude held off the false vengeance."

"Oh." Edison scratched his chin. "I knew that."

Liara smiled. "Of course you did. Let's get going, shall we?"

~~~

Liara reached the top of the dune first.
"Oh, wow."
"What? What is it?" Edison crested the hill.
She didn't answer, but she didn't have to.
Beneath them was not an oasis, but a miniature ecosystem. Several acres of lush greenery, animals, streams, all in the middle of the Libyan Desert. A pocket paradise.

Edison put one hand to his chin. "Yeah, I'm pretty sure the Egg is here somewhere."

Liara rolled her eyes. "Let's head down and find out, shall we?"

Edison following behind her, the two stumbled down the dune toward the tiny Eden before them. The ground beneath their feet
~~~

changed from sand to soil, the temperature dropped from scorching to cool, and they could feel water droplets on their faces. Kangaroo mice and opossums skittered underfoot, while basilisk lizards hid under leaves to avoid the sun and crocodiles rolled over in the river-spring.

The two stood side-by-side, basking in the unexpected glory they had entered. Mule deer and ravens scattered at their intrusion.

Edison moved his hands to his hips and looked around. "If I were an alabaster egg, where would I be?"

"Under an alabaster chicken?"

Edison laughed, looking over at Liara's smug smile. "You always catch me off guard when you do that, you know?"

"I'm glad you don't have me totally figured out, Edison." She tilted her nose to the sky. "It's unseemly for a lady's secrets to be completely revealed, you know."

"All right, fair enough." His words were impatient, but his expression was not. "Where do you think this thing is?"

"Okay." Liara's smile departed in favor of a determined scrunch. "I said that it was supposed to have, what? The leftover creative energies, right?" Edison nodded. "All right, if you have a force radiating out from a point, then it's going to go equally in all directions unless something stops it. Laws of physics."

"And since we have no reason to think otherwise, we can assume that the metaphysical propagates in the same manner." Liara's eyes widened. "Hey," he said, "I know a thing or two about wave and particle physics myself."

She poked him. "Congratulations. So if that's true, our best bet is to look dead-center of this oasis."

"Makes sense." Edison pulled out his cellphone, brushed it off. "Poor baby."

Google Earth. Current location.

SATELLITE IMAGE OBTAINED.

"It's definitely circular."

Calculate center.

CENTER CALCULATED.

Edison walked into the valley, glancing between the screen and the landscape before him. A thick bramble of thorns and burrs slowed him, digging into his skin and clothes, but he fought his way through.

Because his face was covered by his hands,

it was a moment before he realized that he had passed the barrier. There were no large plants here, simply a bed of moss, thick and luxuriant.

Upon this bed lay a stone the size and shape of a chicken egg, but opaline in color, shimmering with reflected light.

Edison paused, his face lit by the radiance. His heartbeat thudded in his chest, strong, clear; the scratches, cuts, and other wounds sustained in the past few days faded, closed, healed. Edison's emotions calmed and his fears vanished.

For just a moment, he forgot why he was here at all; he was lost in the ebb and flow of life that surrounded him. His thinking mind began to sink beneath the primal energy which pulsed and pounded around him.

Then he shook his head, blinked, and laughed, long and loud. All the danger, the madness, the chaos – if he died now, struck down where he stood, it would all be worth it.

I wouldn't trade it for all the peace and safety in the world.

Edison's fingers closed around the Egg. A minor charge flowed through his hand to his heart, raising goosebumps in its path. He pulled; the Egg refused to move. Moss tendrils and roots held fast to the stone, burrowed into its surface like ivy on an old manor.

Edison tugged harder. The plants, the animals, each in their own tongue began to scream; the squirrels scurried over his fingers, biting, trying to make him let go; grasses curled around his feet, yanking, pulling; they begged Edison to let them live, to let the Egg stay.

You take our heart, they cried. *You condemn us to death; we die as you take our life, your hands are stained with our blood.*

Millions of lives pleaded for Edison's mercy and, though tears ran like rivers down his cheeks, he could not, would not, did not, grant it.

At last, the Egg came free. The tendrils which had bound it began to wilt, turning shriveled and brown. The animals began to mourn, chittering and lowing each in their turn. The rot began to spread, but slowly.

Edison forced his way back through the brush, wiping his eyes with the back of his hand. Soon enough, he had reached the other side and found Liara waiting for him.

"Are you okay?" She put a hand on his

shoulder. "Your eyes are really red."

"Allergies." He put on a smile, trying to ignore the death cries around him, behind him. He rubbed his hair with his hand, wiped sweat from his brow.

"Let's go." She did not move, so he repeated it. "Let's go *now*."

"Why? What's…"

"I think Azrael will be here very, very soon." He grabbed her shoulders. "So let's *go*."

Liara took the Egg from Edison. Its surface was pitted by the plant roots which had infiltrated it, but there was an inscription in gold filigree, twisting, changing.

"This is a grimoire!" She tilted the Egg in one direction, then another. "It has spells in it, spells to create life, to trade it, to summon it…"

"Wonderful, fantastic, let's get out of here!" Edison took the Egg back and pocketed it while still looking toward the site it had been in; the decay was starting to spread past the thorn barricades.

Liara swallowed, her eyes flicking back to Edison. "Where?"

"I don't know, I don't know. Just *go*!"

Liara glanced at him once more, then

turned inward, drawing on her new strength, pulling them back to Tripoli.

(*No.*)

She could not reach it. Something

(*I*)

was blocking her, overruling her desires.

...Oreth?

(*Not there.*)

Where then?

There was a weak tug, as if a child was pulling at her hand, unable to move her but strong enough to show her where it wanted her to go.

(*Here.*)

Where's "here?"

(*Here.*)

...Fine. Be unhelpful.

"Hold on tight, Edison," Liara closed her eyes, and, once again, they were gone.

~~~

"Where the hell are we?" asked Edison. There was little light, and what there was seemed diluted, filtered, as it came through the windows. The walls were solid stone, carved rather than cut, and there were no furnishings
~~~

in the hallway to speak of.

Liara did not reply; she was staring at the gilt double-doors in front of her, at the end of the hall. The pull was stronger now, more insistent; Liara found her right hand rising to the door and had to hold it in place with her left.

Edison glanced over and had a strange moment of déjà-vu; for just a second, he would have sworn that he could see Oreth's form overlaying Liara's.

"Liara. What's going on?"

Her teeth were clenched as she struggled to hold her place. "I think that Oreth wants us to go through this door."

"Umm...okay." Edison leaned toward the door, then looked back at Liara. "Why aren't we?"

"We don't even know what's behind there!" Her hand lunged for the door.

"Liara, if Oreth wants you to go through that door, I think you should. Let go of him."

Liara stared at Edison for a few seconds, then released her hand, which flew to and opened the double doors.

The room beyond was small. A few torches in sconces provided light, and there were some chairs, but the most prominent furnishing was the table in the center of the room.

Also, it was where the smell was coming from.

Upon this table lay a skeleton, bones cracked, and looking centuries old. Any putrefaction should have been long over, yet there it was; a terrible smell of rot and death that lingered in both their nostrils and their spirits.

Liara scanned the corpse, not voicing the fear she felt clawing at her throat. At the body's waist, she found what she had hoped

(*feared*)

to see. She took it.

Oreth's trowel.

"Well done," came the resonating voice of Azrael from the open door. He clapped his hands once, twice, thrice. He slipped into the room, closing the double doors behind him. Liara braced herself for the draining effect of Azrael's aura.

"I'm glad you came." Azrael stopped his advance, pausing about five feet from them. He turned his head to Liara. "Is it true? Do you have his Nature? Did he somehow send it to you?"

Liara licked her lips, thought about lying. Didn't.

"Yes." She raised her head high. "He sent it to me, and I am keeping it safe for him."

Azrael laughed. His suit seemed to glow slightly. "Keeping it safe? Oreth has, unfortunately, passed on...and by his own choice, I might add." Azrael took another step toward them, and seemed to glow even brighter. His eyes narrowed, flicking between Liara and Edison.

I should be crumpling now. She kept waiting for the agony to hit, but she felt neither pain nor fatigue. "We'll see. Just let us take him and we'll go."

"Oh, I don't think so," chuckled Azrael. "You see, I need you now. I was to share my Nature with Oreth to make myself...safe. Approachable again." He smiled. "Now that you have the Nature, *you* can help me instead. And live, of course."

(*Make him angry*)

Liara cocked a hip and tapped her lips with a finger. "Hmm...how about a counteroffer?" she asked, her eyes alight. "How about I take Oreth with me, and you...go fuck yourself?" Despite the seriousness of the situation, Edison snickered.

Azrael sighed. "I don't see why this is so hard for the two of you to understand," he said. "I want to stop killing things. No more catastrophes in shopping malls or on school campuses simply because I decide to drop by. No more mass deforestations or sudden swellings of red algal tides killing fish if I go out for a swim. I should be commended for this, not condemned."

"What's the matter, Azrael?" Liara crossed her arms and turned her face away from him. "Can't deal with who you are anymore? For God's sake, you're like a child whining about being short or something." She looked back at the angry incarnation of Death. "The whole world shouldn't suffer just because you can't keep it in your pants."

Azrael's voice dropped an octave and his chin dipped down a fraction of an inch. "This is your last warning, Liara. Join the Nature with me, or I will kill you and take it from another."

"Oh, no, me boyo!" Edison hopped up to center stage as Azrael trained venomous eyes upon him. "I don't think you'll be murderin' anyone t'day, don'tchaknow?"

"Your frivolity is unamusing, Edison. This is between Liara and myself. Step back."

"Or what? You'll kill me?" Edison smirked, getting into it. "Get a new threat, broken record boy. You...are...boring...me." Edison punctuated each word of the last sentence with a tap on Azrael's chest. Sweat was coating his back, sticking to his shirt, but he hoped that Azrael wouldn't see.

Azrael tilted his head, first one way, then the other, like a scientist investigating a particularly strange anomaly.

"Fine." Azrael turned his gaze back on Liara. "If you don't cooperate, woman, this is but a sample of what shall befall you." His hand came up, two fingers raised to the heavens, thumb curled in the ancient gesture of Ending.

"No!" Liara dived, moving to interpose herself as Azrael intoned his spell.

<<Into the void, with emptiness as your comfort and nonexistence as your bread. I consign you to Death.>> Azrael's hand curled into a fist, knuckles whitening.

<<Begone.>>

Edison closed his eyes, waiting for the

strike, for the life to leave his body, for his soul to depart, for...

Wait a minute. I'm still thinking?

He cracked an eyelid, and saw, surrounding himself and Liara, a nebulous green sphere, holding shadows of trees, elephants, turtles, and other creatures which he did not or could not identify. These figures swirled and struggled against the force outside, an unending tide of dark horsemen that threw themselves at the verdant barrier and dissipated like dreams.

Liara's and Azrael's faces looked just as surprised as he felt. He shook his head.

"What the hell?" Then, as he turned back toward Azrael, he felt a soothing warmth in his pocket.

Could it be...

He drew out the Egg, feeling it crackle beneath his fingers. He marveled at the shimmering rainbow colors, the thrum which vibrated within, the pulsing of the universe's heart.

Edison's eyes met Azrael's and, therein, Edison saw something he had never thought to see within that darkness.

Confusion. Awe. Terror.

Edison held the Egg out before him, a priest in a vampire movie warding off evil with his holy symbol. He looked right, ensuring that Liara was enveloped within the Egg's field, then took a step forward.

Edison felt tangible pressure, like he was forcing his legs to push him through water as Azrael's face transformed from fear to anger.

"No. You shall not have him." He extended both hands, set his feet, and began repeating his chant, invoking primal Death, stemming the tide of creation with destruction.

The aura flickered and flared, but Edison stepped again, one foot after the other. Azrael appeared to be buckling under the pressure, going to one knee, struggling to keep his hands raised.

I'm doing it. Edison's heart was racing, adrenaline turning his muscles into tight ropes of steel. *I'm beating Azrael...we're going to make it! We're going to...*

Azrael's eyes flashed. Keeping one hand held aloft, he drew a knife from his pocket, flicked it open, then slid the blade of the knife across his wrist. Blood, black, slick like oil, coated the blade.

Edison halted his advance, and Liara recoiled.

"What is he doing?"

Edison licked his lips and focused on keeping the barrier in place. "I don't know!"

He took another step; he was almost close enough to grab Oreth's corpse.

Azrael's knife dripped blood. He held it by the hilt, waving it in the air, chanting.

Then he threw it at Edison's left eye.

"Shit!" Edison dodged, ducking under the knife. It was soon apparent that the knife was only the distraction - the lapse of concentration left him vulnerable to the sudden bull-rush Azrael utilized, diving and swiping at Edison's hand.

Harendar appeared, carving a flaming arc which brushed Azrael's suit coat, singeing and smoking, as the Egg ricocheted off the stone walls, clattering against the floor and landing next to the entryway, its light fading, its power gone.

Without the protection of the Egg, the full strength of Azrael's aura hit, shattering the rings on Liara's hands and driving both of them to the ground. Edison's eyes widened as he saw old wounds on his hands begin to reopen.

"Are we done?" Azrael stood and brushed off his sleeves, then adjusted his suit. "Good. I admit that I was caught by surprise. Well played," He smiled, circling around them as he spoke, his teeth gleaming in the torchlight. "Unfortunately, this means that both of you will have to die, as I cannot let you spread this knowledge, this...vulnerability of mine, to anyone." His face regained its emotionless appearance.

Edison could not speak. He felt as he had after Marathon, on the verge of death, exhausted. Even his Nature seemed far away and untouchable.

He strained to turn his head toward Liara, and he saw she was looking back at him, tears refracting the green in her eyes.

Liara's lips moved.

I love you.

Edison smiled, tried to respond.

I love you too. I'm sorry.

Azrael knelt down and laid his hands on both Essentials. They squirmed in pain at his touch. "Any last words?"

"How about, 'shut the fuck up?'" came a

woman's voice from the door. Azrael's hands lifted and his head snapped back to see Eriana, head held high and black hair merging with shimmering black satin, silhouetted against the entry.

In her hand was the Alabaster Egg. She was smiling.

"Eriana." Azrael, stood, backing away. "Put that down."

Her smile widened. "Umm...no. No, I don't think so."

Azrael's eyes blazed hot. "You betray *me*, bitch?" The ground underneath his feet splintered into shards of stone.

"*You* betrayed *me*." Eriana walked, moving toward the table surrounded by Essentials. "You tricked me, had me attack those I had no cause against..." The green shimmer of the Alabaster egg erupted, shielding the two prostrate forms and releasing them from Azrael's power. They scrambled to their feet, clasping hands.

"And I'm *done*. You made me, made *Vengeance,* into your own personal slave. I am *nobody's* bitch, you understand, you gangrenous, decayed fuck!"

Azrael smiled, cold and hard, like ice, like

diamond. "Yes, Eriana, you are. Can you protect them? No, your Nature is to *avenge*, not *protect*. Sooner or later, you will leave them...and then, who takes your jewel? Who is left without the protection?" He spread his hands.

"None escape Death. Not now, not ever. Choose your time, if you like, but I will come for you."

Azrael's words echoed through the room; to Eriana and Liara, the echo was merely the result of sound waves bouncing off the walls and reinforcing one another.

To Edison, lord of all Communication, Azrael's words resonated with prophecy.

Azrael stepped forward and pressed his hand against the field. It sparked and singed, steam and smoke rising. His hand began to crisp, the skin on the ends of his fingers erupting into small flames. Azrael's brows furrowed and his teeth bared.

The lush, green aura coruscating from the Egg began to blacken, to rot, in creeping tendrils from his hand; they were inching, yes, and it was a struggle, but Azrael was winning. If he could hold up.

Eriana's eyes widened, then flicked to Oreth's corpse, then to Liara.

She remembered the look on Oreth's face when he had left her. Saw it, for the first time, unclouded by the heartbreak it had caused her. Saw the regret in his eyes as he did what he thought he *had* to do. Heard his words once again. ALL of them.

"A god must not be held back by a mortal love." He took her hands in his and kissed them as she cried, her eyes streaming and red. She could not speak. His eyes were red as well, but set, determined to do what he thought he must. His voice cracked as he continued.

"Neither should a mortal be shackled to the greatness of a god. Be free, Eriana, and be happy." He turned away from her and traveled to some distant place, far from her, far from what had been his home for so long.

For the first time in history, in the hundreds of years they had known of each other, Eriana saw Liara for who she *truly* was; a woman, like any other, who had fallen in love with a man who had not loved her.

And she saw herself, the part of herself mired in pain and rage, for the blind fool she had been.

"Take care of him." She threw the Egg toward the stunned woman. Then she smiled.

Liara caught it, snatched the stone from the air, nodded.

"Good luck, Eriana." Liara gathered Oreth and Edison in her arms. Azrael lunged toward them, but Eriana twisted her hands in his suit jacket, hurling him against the wall, cracks running out from the impact site like rivers.

Liara focused, drawing once more on the Nature of the man whose skeleton lay in her arms, the man who the woman covering their retreat still loved.

Only love can engender such rage.

~~~

Azrael drew himself up, assessing Eriana as she did him, the two standing across the room from one another, moving in a circle.

"Is this how it is, then?"

Eriana nodded.

"You know you can't win."

She nodded again. "Perhaps, evil one, all I can do is make sure that you remember my
~~~

name, and die forgiven for my wasted immortality."

"Perhaps, Eriana." Azrael paused. "For what it is worth, I had hoped that it would never come to this."

"Forgive me if I don't find that particularly comforting just now."

The two stood, frozen in stark relief, the white suit and black dress contrasting each other.

Azrael raised his hands, and a necrotic wave of power thrust toward Eriana, dissolving wood and splintering stone in its path.

Eriana made no attempt to dodge. The power impacted her with a low rumble, like an underground detonation.

Her supple skin began to wither and slough away; her flesh almost bubbled as her hair first whitened and then drifted to the ground in a perverse rain. Her eyes clouded over with cataracts, blinding her; cancerous growths sprouted in her lymph nodes, her breasts, her throat.

Still, Eriana managed a smile, rotting teeth falling from receding gums. Azrael advanced on her decaying form.

"Vengeance cannot survive Death, you fool."

"Not vengeance. Never supposed to be vengeance. Only..." Her voice trailed off in a series of wheezing coughs.

Azrael's eyebrow cocked. "What was that?" He leaned over towards her desiccated, ruined body. "Say it again."

Eriana's eyes rolled up as the flesh withered away from the sockets like old wallpaper. Still, her voice resounded through the room like an atomic detonation.

<<JUSTICE!>>

Fire blazed within her, in her eyes, mouth, nose; the fire consumed the decaying flesh and bones until it was all that remained. This fire, an inferno in human shape, enveloped Azrael, coating him in blood-flames, searing him with soul-flames.

He began to scream.

~~~

Outskirts of Baghdad. 2 A.M. People staring. Liara huffed as she ran down the streets, a skeleton over one shoulder, held together by
~~~

desiccated ligaments and shreds of fabric, and a very jostled godling on the other.

"Why...are...you...running?"   Edison's words were punctuated by impacts to his chest.

Liara didn't answer. There was no answer – the Nature, Oreth's Nature, was calling her and there could be no refusal, no delay. Down the alley. Through the door. Occupants scream-ing – no matter, sorry – to the basement, here, HERE!

Liara flung Edison off her shoulder and laid Oreth's bones on the ground. From her Otherspace she pulled Oreth's trowel and the Alabaster Egg. The runes on the Egg swirled, then stabilized.

"Edison, watch the door."

Edison picked himself off the floor. "What?"

"The door, Edison. Please."

Edison looked up the basement stairs. The Iraqi man of the house had a baseball bat in one hand and was screaming at them in Arabic.

<<You get out of here! Get out of my house!>>

Edison walked upward, hands open to show he held nothing in them, trying his best to look nonthreatening.

<<Sir, let me explain...>>

Liara blocked them out. This must be done. The instructions were here. The materials were here. It was his only hope.

She took the Egg and laid it in Oreth's chest, where his heart would have been.

The man at the top of the stairs swung his bat at Edison's head, still screaming admonitions and demanding that they leave.

<<No! No! You get out of here! I called the police!>>

<<Sir, stay calm...>>. Edison ducked just in time to avoid the strike.

Liara produced a small knife and nicked her wrist, allowing the blood to dribble down onto the Egg, which turned a deep crimson-green and started to crackle.

<<Blood for man, the mortal half, held in the blood and begat by the blood.>> The chant echoed, a deep bass resonating through her soul.

She reached over and scooped up a handful of dirt floor, sprinkling it over Oreth's corpse. <<Soil from home, the place of the Second Birth, a reminder of who you are and how you

came to be.>>

The trowel she placed in his hand, wrapping his bony fingers around it.

<<A symbol of the god, the work that was done and the work that calls you back.>>

Liara leaned in to Oreth's grinning skull, and breathed into his mouth, whispering, <<The Breath of Life, the first breath given that you might breathe again.>> In that breath, the white fire of the life Oreth had sent her, his soul, his Nature, leapt from her to the shell lying on the earth.

Freed from the compulsion which had driven her, Liara stumbled backward, pressing her wrist to stop the bleeding.

The Alabaster Egg began to pulse, throwing a red light onto the basement walls. A dark slime started to spread over the Egg as creepers curled out, tapping into the splatters of blood, rooting through the dirt, then driving into the bones surrounding it. Veins and muscles raced along those tendrils, sprung from nothing to sheathe white scaffolding in bloody red meat. The pulsing of the Egg began to resemble the lub-dub of a heartbeat as the pectoral muscles closed over it; nerves stretched out from the reconstructed brain to light up the channels of sense and motion.

Oreth's eyes opened as the last of his dark skin wrapped itself around the fingers clutching the trowel, and a sharp inhalation heralded his return to life.

Liara's eyes were tearing as she watched the resurrection of an old friend, an old love, one for whom she had grieved many times, and one who had sacrificed himself for her.

"Welcome back, Oreth."

~~~

Death was coming for Oreth, and he could not escape it.

Oreth's mind fixated on the figure marching toward him: Azrael, the Essential of Death and most feared of all the immortal beings on Earth. For centuries, Azrael had been withdrawing more and more, appearing only rarely, and then always accompanied by death tolls numbering in the hundreds or thousands. Some of the younger Essentials even entertained the idea that Azrael didn't exist at all, that he was just a Bogeyman myth
~~~

for what passed for Essential society.

Oreth was not a young Essential. Oreth knew better.

Azrael wanted something from Oreth; he had tried reasoning, he had tried bargaining, and he had tried threatening, and still Oreth had refused to tie Death to Cities.

There were not many things that Oreth was willing to die for. He swallowed, watching Azrael as he came closer; the elder Essential's face was almost cheerful, foreseeing an end to his long-lasting predicament. Oreth closed his eyes.

This was worth dying for; Cities would not be polluted thus by <u>his</u> hand.

Oreth felt his arms being grasped, felt himself being pulled along the ground. He forced his eyes open; Roman legionnaires had taken hold of him and were dragging him away from the battlefield, toward the city itself, calling out for help, help for the god.

Oreth could no longer see Azrael, but he could feel his presence. Azrael was running now, fearful of losing his chance, perhaps. Oreth didn't know, and could barely care.

One of the legionnaires fell, his limbs sud-

denly turning leprous and withered; the other stumbled at the increase in weight, but re-gained his footing and ran on. He shouted commands to the legionnaires around him, and they formed up into a miniature phalanx, covering his retreat.

The soldier managed to cross the invisible boundary into the city of Rome itself; to Oreth, it felt as if his body was electrified, and the weights pressing on him were lifted. Once again, Oreth was a god, and he stood upright to the cheers of those who could see him.

The defending phalanx melted away, screaming, dying, and Azrael stood at the border of Rome, his dark eyes burning with anger, with hatred.

"I will have it." He spat the words into the air. "I will be free." He stepped forward into the city.

Oreth assessed his own strength and that of his enemy. His heart sank, but he was not surprised.

He could not win. He was not strong enough. Not even here.

Oreth knelt, kissed the ground of Rome, and watered it with his tears.

"Forgive me."

He Moved, sending himself to the barely-civilized lands which would one day be called Tlatilco, behind a rude tent pitched against the wind.

It was a city. No one could see him here if he did not wish them to.

Oreth had heard Azrael's scream of rage as he disappeared, and knew that Azrael would soon be venting his frustration on the people and city of Rome, and that the Empire would fall.

Oreth shed his armor, his weapons, everything that distinguished him from a normal man; he removed his clothing, his jewels. Before dropping his knife, he shaved his hair with it.

"Every connection, every trace." His words came sing-song as he worked. "Every connection, every trace." He held his ancient bronze trowel, caressing it with his hands, as his only possession.

Naked and shorn, Oreth focused once more, this time transporting himself back to his home, to his city of origin, where he had received the Nature. It was desolate, deserted since its people had been deported and the province to which it belonged annexed by the Persians, but it still meant something to Oreth, who could see each structure which had ever stood as if it were newly built.

Oreth collapsed into the dirt, the sand rough against his naked flesh. Azrael would find him again, Oreth knew.

"If I give in, then he destroys Cities. If I do not, he kills me and finds the next, and then destroys Cities through them. I cannot stop him. I only pray that someone finds a way before he finds me."

In the exact spot where he had had his Second Birth, Oreth plunged his bronze trowel into the ground. This time, instead of receiving insight and power, Oreth poured himself into that trowel; he poured his memories, his hopes, his fears, and his desires into it, the parts of himself that made him <u>him</u> so that Azrael could not sense him, would not be able to see him.

He collapsed onto the ground, unconscious, and would remain there for many days. When Azrael arrived, searching for him, trying to follow his trail, Oreth was still lying in the dirt, his breathing almost stilled.

Azrael did not see him. After all, he was looking for a god, not a corpse.

PART THREE

17 – FACTS OF LIFE

"Slow down, slow down. Eriana did *what?*" Oreth's eyes were wide over his cup of coffee.

The three were back in New York City, around a Denny's table covered in food and coffee cups. Oreth had been possessed of a tremendous appetite, and had eaten as much as three normal people.

Liara's eyes were wet with the tears of remembrance. "It's true." Edison nodded as she continued. "She bailed us out back there.

Stalled Azrael so we could get out."

"Yeah." Edison smiled. "She looked like she was about to carve herself a chunk of Death-God, lemme tell ya."

"Damn." Oreth bowed his head and rubbed his forehead. Several moments passed in awkward silence as he adjusted items on the table, straightening fork and knife. He brushed a few crumbs off his turquoise sleeve – Liara had re-fitted them all once they had returned – then looked back at the other Essentials, his steady voice a sharp contrast to the redness in his eyes.

"Well, what now?"

Both of his companions blinked at him across the table. Edison shook his head. "What do you mean?"

Oreth pointed up at the widescreen television near their table.

"Iranian and Israeli governments are accusing each other of the detonation which occurred over the Dead Sea today, resulting in hundreds dead and thousands with serious injuries." The newscaster had visible circles under his eyes, and his hair looked in need of a brush.

"The settlements of Ein Gedi and Neve Zohar escaped damage from the blast, due to what scientists are calling 'dispersive wind phenomena,' but the rest of the area within a five-mile radius of the Dead Sea was decimated. As you can see from these satellite photos, the destruction is close to total." The anchor took a drink of water before continuing. "The Israeli government claims that Iran, using its allies in the Hezbollah and Hamas terrorist organizations, delivered an experimental weapon designed to deliver a high-power blast with no detectable fallout. President Ahmadinejad of Iran has denied this accusation, calling it 'another fantasy' from the 'Zionist regime' and claiming that, if anything has occurred, it is merely a setup by Netanyahu designed to trigger international intervention in Middle Eastern affairs. The United States issued a statement that..."

"Azrael isn't dead." Oreth's voice drew the attention of the others back to him. "I'd stake my life on that...again." Sip of coffee. "The problem is this, I think – Death has grown too strong in him. It consumes everything around him, lashes out at his slightest loss of control."

"Despoina said something like that." They turned to Edison as he spoke. "She told me that Azrael had linked their Natures together, and that it was kind of a..." His hands rolled in the air as he groped for the phrase, "...a pressure valve? Does that make sense?"

Oreth nodded. "That's what he wanted to do with Cities." He paused, frowning, thinking. "Perhaps Despoina's Nature didn't have enough life in it to satiate Death's hunger, and so he still needed me; maybe it was just too much time. I don't know."

He leaned forward on his elbows. "Here's what I *do* know. Azrael has been Death since before the rest of us came about – the first humans." He paused to let this sink in. "What if he's not *supposed* to live that long?" The others glanced at each other, then back at him, their brows furrowed. He went on. "We know we're immortal – we live forever, we heal, all that. What if he's not supposed to? Death is a part of the cycle of life, back and forth. What if, because he *is* Death, he's supposed to..."

"..to die?" Liara's voice was soft, quiet. Oreth nodded.

"Exactly. We exemplify our Natures, and

our Natures, us. What if the bleeding of Azrael's power is because Death itself is angry at him?"

Edison's brow creased. "When we were facing Azrael, he said something...something about how nothing could hide from Death. It sounded like...well." He chuckled and a blush crept up his cheeks. "I know it sounds silly, but it sounded like...a prophecy."

Oreth tilted his head. "Have you ever heard an actual prophecy before?"

Edison nodded.

"Believe it or not, the oracle at Delphi was known to issue true prophecies now and again; I went down there because I was interested in listening to the prophetess speak, wanted to see if I could understand her words. I could...and they were right. Not that the interpretations given by the priestesses were anything like what she actually would say, but...anyway, I got the same kind of shiver listening to them as I did when Azrael said that."

"Well, if he's at war with Death itself...that would assume that Death is an actual being, with a consciousness of its own, wouldn't it?" Liara wiggled her hand in a see-saw motion.

"I'm not sure if I can buy into that."

Edison lifted his sandwich. "Not necessarily. It could just be like a dam, water building up behind it until it overflows." He looked at Oreth. "And if Death is at war with itself...what could that do to the planet? To everything?"

Oreth's smile was grim. *Back for three hours and I'm already committing suicide.*

"We need to kill Azrael." The words fell from his lips like notes from the Trump of Doom. "We have to release Death, let the Nature pass to another."

Silence blanketed the table, the only sound the humming of the fan and the yammering of the television ads.

"How would we do that?" Edison swallowed his bite of turkey and rye. "Everyone that I've ever met is terrified of him. All the stories say he's invincible."

"He's not invincible." Everyone stopped and looked at Liara. "He was bleeding after I hit him with Harendar. You saw Eriana throw him into the wall. His fingers caught fire when he pressed against the Egg. It hurt him; it just didn't *stop* him."

"Okay, okay...so, what, we hit him with a

nuke? Would that do it?"

Oreth shook his head. "Remember, he's *Death*. He can repudiate, reject it. Liara can take a battleship apart with one blow of her hammer; you can unmake a cellphone network with a thought. Azrael *undoes* Death. We can't kill him as long as he can command his Nature. And, as long as he is still...overloaded, I guess, we can't even really get near him – especially now that Despoina is dead and he is no longer tied to the Ways."

"Great – so, we knock him out? Chloroform him? I'm not overly excited about our options here, guys." Edison shook his head and downed his coffee. "I mean, we can't kill him, we can't get close to him...what *can* we do?"

Liara laughed. "We don't beat Death by fighting him in a duel...well, not usually. Remember the Labyrinth? How did you get us to the center?"

"By connecting us to the outside, making it a real place."

"Why did that work?"

"Um...because if it was a real place, I could GPS it."

"No." Oreth tapped on the table to emphasize his point. "It was because a real place has to go *somewhere.* You used *your* Nature to overwrite one of her basic laws."

Liara nodded. "So, if we can somehow tie Azrael to something that prevents him from denying Death, we can kill him?"

"That's my working theory." Oreth sighed. "There's only one Essential I can think of who can do that, and she doesn't exactly hang out in the spotlight."

"Who?"

"She doesn't have a name, not one she tells us, anyway. Her Nature came to her a few millennia ago – I remember hearing stories about her, traveling, performing 'miracles.'"

"Wait." Edison put his cup down and leaned forward. "You mean...the Matron?"

"Exactly." Oreth nodded and reached for the sugar. "The Matron, holder of the genitive Essence – Life itself."

"How could she help us?" Liara turned her head from one to the other of her companions. "And would she be willing to?"

"I get it!" Edison slapped his forehead with the heel of his hand, laughed, then paused, looking at Liara.

Liara thought, her lips tight and her fingers tapping her water glass. After a few moments, she looked up.

"If something is alive, it can be killed!" Her outburst sounded out over the restaurant, drawing the glances of several nearby patrons.

"Shh! Exactly my thought – if we can convince the Matron to help us, then she might be able to force mortality on Azrael." Oreth paused, licked his lips. "Of course, if it doesn't work, then we all die. Azrael has made a miscalculation or two of late – he's not likely to do so again."

Edison laughed. "I know! He totally hasn't read the Evil Overlord list. I mean, letting the big doomsday weapon, your weakness, roll away...and *not* picking it up yourself? Totally Evil Overlord *Epic* fail. You know what I mean?"

Both Oreth and Liara were staring at Edison, shaking their heads. Liara put one hand over his. "No, Edison. We have *no* idea what you mean, but that's okay. We love you anyway." She leaned in and kissed his cheek.

There was a moment of silence, punctuated by shy glances, before Oreth cleared his throat.

"I think we need to move fast. I don't know what Eriana can do to hold Azrael up." He glanced down, inhaled, looked back up. His voice cracked as he continued. "She's probably dead by now, and the fight's over. How long is it going to take him to be back on his feet and looking for us?" He met his two companions' gazes across the table, and they nodded, faces pale.

Liara raised one hand a bit. "I guess I'll be the one to ask the question, but do we know where the Matron is? Can we get hold of her?"

"Well..." Oreth trailed off, and there was a moment where the other two leaned in, waiting for him to continue.

"...I have no fucking clue." Another pause, and then the three companions started laughing, great peals of it that seemed out of place, prompting their waitress to bang the coffee pot on their table and demand that they "shut yer traps, yer botherin' the other customers!"

Oreth wiped the tears from his eyes, stood. "Mabel, I know you're having a rough day. Let me tell you, though – customer service is not your strong suit." Mabel gaped at him like a fish, and the other Essentials watched, their eyes moving from one to the other, slight grins still on their faces.

He placed a hand on Mabel's shoulder. "I'm sorry, but I think you should take up a new line of work. Run for office maybe. Maybe a judge." He nodded. "A court would suit you."

"Mister, I..."

"Shh." He put a finger to her lips. "You'll make a good judge, Mabel." He beckoned his compatriots, and they began to file out of the restaurant. At the door, Oreth turned.

"Oh, and you should stop holding that grudge against your grandmother. It's not her fault – she was just trying her best."

The door closed behind Oreth as he emerged to joyful smiles.

"Why did you do that?" He turned to Liara as she spoke "Not that I'm upset, but...well, you didn't need to, did you? I mean, it wasn't all that important..."

"It's not?" Oreth arched an eyebrow. "I disagree. I had the privilege, recently, of living and dying as an ordinary man, several, several times, actually, and each time that ordinary man was unaware of anything special about himself, except that he heard voices, that he moved from place to place." He spread his hands. "For all he knew, he was insane. But human, still; always human.

"Humanity is what we're all about, isn't it?" Oreth pointed at each of them in turn. "Cities, the Forge, Communication – if we ignore the race that birthed us, what are we?" He swept his arm outward, encompassing New York in its arc. "Humanity built this, and it makes me strong. If I neglect them – and I have, I know – then my heart grows as cold as their fires, my eyes as dim as their hopes. Never again." His voice rose with his color. "Never again will I do this. *I* am not important. The Nature is. I always knew that, but I was like Azrael; I was obsessed with the idea that the Nature had come to me, *me*, that I couldn't imagine it passing to anyone else."

A bus pulled up. Number 41. Rob's bus, of course.

"You...you remember now?" Liara glanced away from Oreth's face, her hand tightening around Edison's fingers.

Oreth paused, his hand on the assist rail, and looked back. "Not everything, but most – and more all the time. It's like the Egg healed my mind along with my brain." He shook his head, laughing. "It's been so long since my mind has been whole, I almost don't know what to do with it all."

Oreth turned back in to the bus and shook Rob's hand. The other two followed.

Rob shook his head as the trio entered his bus. "What crazy shit are we in for today?"

"Nothin' big." Edison clapped the larger man's shoulder before moving to his seat. "Just off to kill Death."

Rob laughed. "Sounds like a party. Billy Idol alright for ya?"

INTERLUDE

Azrael writhed in the grip of the fire searing his flesh and his soul. But for his mastery of his Nature, he would have died minutes

(*hours? centuries? millennia?*)

ago. He would not. Death stood waiting for his command, its bony hand outstretched, but even in this agony he moved forward, refusing its cold, comforting embrace.

Each death – and there were many – echoed in his screaming flesh; those given justly were a momentary balm, but were far outnumbered by the needless, the careless, the callous. The potential sum of these lives had been translated into suffering.

And he was not clear of it yet.

Azrael struggled to his feet, the fire turning the sand around him to molten glass, heat radiating from him in great pulses of sunflare. Step by grueling step he approached the port, filled with fishermen and their children on boats, wealthy tourists and residents taking their yachts. With yet another fragment of his will, Azrael cloaked himself with the *Nizra'el*, the Obscuring Chant, hiding his torment from the views of the mortals. He stopped, feeling his aura lashing for them, Death begging to claim their lives. At the same time, he knew that murdering them would only add to his torment. Eriana's vengeance was powerful and well-conceived.

<<Mommy...>> A little girl whose parents were prepping their boat for sailing followed his progress with her eyes. <<Is that the Devil?>>

<<Quiet, Angela; Mommy's working.>>
<<Look, Mommy, look!>>

A well-conceived vengeance indeed, thought Azrael, but insufficient to the task. He was the oldest of Essentials, the longest-lived, and he knew more about magic than all of the others combined. All he needed was an innocent soul.

As a starting point.

He smiled, flames scorching his teeth and tongue. "Hello, Angela."

18 – LIFE AND DEATH

Oreth, Liara, and Edison waited as the tour guide explained the importance of their location.

"The United Nations headquarters is located on an 18-acre site and is composed of four major buildings. It is an international zone, controlling its own police force, and..."

"The biggest metaphysical construction project in history." Edison's eyes were roving the compound. "Designed to bring together disparate representatives of world cultures for discussion and mediation." He held his hands out like a magician showing off his final performance. "It feels like I'm in a warm saltwater pool, floating away effortlessly."

Oreth nodded. "We need to get away from this tour, get into the Assembly chamber."

Liara tapped him on the shoulder. "Why didn't you just bring us in there, Oreth?"

"Didn't you hear the tour guide?" His smile was evident in his tone. "It's not a city. It's an international zone."

Liara nodded. "Fair enough. You heard the man, Edison. Distraction time."

He grinned. "I'm on it. Tower of Babel redux, coming right up."

"...if you'll look this way, you'll see afed glap eyred..."

The crowd surrounding the tour guide began to murmur as her words were garbled, then to yell at each other as they realized it was happening to them. Arguments in various new forms of gibberish turned to screams, shouts, and general chaos.

During the commotion, three members of the tour vanished.

They scurried toward the General Assembly chambers, sidestepping the guards who had rushed out to investigate the sudden commotion on the grounds. The three Essentials ducked through hallways and double doors until they reached the Chamber of the Assembly.

The huge golden monolith which stood at the front of the room dwarfed the rows of seats which would be occupied by politicians and delegates, all jockeying for favor from allies and potential patrons; the room was filled with the corruption of nations, a corruption which squelched between the toes. Still...

"It has to be here." Edison closed his eyes. "Not only is this place wired to the gills, it *speaks*."

Oreth nodded, smiling. "Men and women from around the world come here to negotiate, to form a single body of law and order. If we can't reach out from here, we'll never find her."

"Sounds good, boys." Liara was perched atop the monument. "I don't know how long the runes are going to hold, you know — this thing isn't Armetium, after all, and *I* didn't make it." She smiled. "So, after I give the word, make it fast, all right? We really don't want to be hanging around when it collapses."

Oreth clasped Edison's hand. "Are you ready?"

Edison grinned and clapped Oreth's shoulder. "Lighten up, man; this is *hardly* the most dangerous thing we're planning to do today." Then he took out his cellphone and moved around, glancing at the screen as he walked, looking for the best reception spot. "Got it."

Oreth stood in the center of the room, looking toward the monolith, arms raised. He nodded to Liara.

Liara returned his nod and went to work. With Harendar, sized now to fit in one hand, and a chisel in the other, she set to carving a series of words, written in the tongue of the metal and of those who forge it. These were the strongest of such runes that she knew – *Lithlenum*, sign of omnipotence; *Elfer*, sign of omniscience; *Ganor*, sign of omnipresence. Each of these signs was enough, in itself, to sink a fleet, to destroy an army, to shape a nation, if used correctly; together, the three sigils formed the triple triangle of the Eternal, channeling the Universe's power into the vessel.

Immediately, the carvings began to sag in

on themselves, the power within them melting the metal, threatening to distort and destroy the runes...with disastrous consequences.

"Go! Go!" Liara dropped her chisel and laid her hand on the monument, channeling her strength into the metal, which had started to glow like a miniature sun.

Edison's fingers were plugging at his cell phone, clicks blurring together into one constant hum as he linked his device to each and every network on the planet – top secret, CB radio, every phone and every camera was his. The power of the Eternal cast the images into a great projection, ghostly figures and landscapes filling the Assembly chamber, almost giving them substance. The Essentials could hear the voices, see the messages being sent.

Edison handed his phone to Oreth, who clasped the beacon and held it high. He reached out – for the first time in almost two thousand years, *really* reached out – and called to his Nature, channeling that call through the Eternal's sigil.

His message was simple, and he felt each city responding to it.

Where is she?

His consciousness stretched, fusing with the souls of civilizations, searching over time, over space...

"Hurry up, guys! We've got meltdown in less than a minute!"

So many. Oreth's mind was flooded with information. *So many of them now...*

Edison, his task complete, watched as the golden pillar began to radiate rainbow colors, casting strange shadows on the wall, shadows of things that were not in the room with them.

Sydney. London. Paris. Moscow...hurry, hurry...

"We need to get out of here, Oreth!" Edison ran up to his friend's side, his voice at the edge of Oreth's hearing.

Cambodia. Tibet. "Almost, not yet..." People were pulling on his sleeves, trying to get him out of the room.

Cork...Dublin...YES!

Oreth opened his eyes to the blinding vision of the golden monolith burning, scorching his pupils and searing his skull.

"Come on!" The overloaded power began jetting from the mauled sigil, setting walls aflame and smashing podia and benches. Liara leapt from her perch and rolled to Oreth's side, as Edison wrapped his arms around them both.

Oreth grabbed onto his destination and pulled them out as the room collapsed in atomic fire.

~~~

Waterford, Ireland. Oreth breathed in, exhaled; it was always a relief to be back in a city, and the marquee on City Hall saluted him with a *Hello, Father! Welcome home!* which he felt, but did not see, and which sent confusion through the passing pedestrians. The port community was filled to the brim with people working, playing, eating, laughing. The group had appeared in a tavern, of which there were many, and their appearance sparked no more curiosity than a waitress asking if they had been served yet. The trio took up seats at a table near the door, and Oreth settled in, closing his eyes and folding his hands together.

Matron. Oreth beckoned, sending the message through all of the city conduits – public phones rang, newspaper headlines changed, messengers went looking for someone they
~~~

didn't know.

Liara and Edison stepped out the door, scanning the streets, looking for someone, *anyone*, who might possess the most basic and powerful Nature of all. Children, men, women, all mortal, some sidling away, some oblivious, and some distracted by other matters.

Time stretched on. Five minutes. Ten.

"...Oreth?" Liara's eyes were flicking around the cityscape. "Are you...sure she's here?"

Oreth nodded, his eyes narrowed and his face tight. "She's here."

He rose from his seat. "Follow me."

The three marched through the streets. Oreth focused, never looking to the side; Liara and Edison waved, smiled, and tried very hard *not* to look like terrorists or psychopaths. The local citizenry gave them a wide berth, with only a few in the way long enough to warrant an "excuse me."

Oreth led the group down the streets to a small bakery, decorated with enticing pictures of pastries and displaying cinnamon rolls and muffins in the large show window. Gracie's Buns and Cakes.

He pushed the door open, revealing a comfortable-looking shop. It was small, but the aroma was rich, almost tangible. Warm lights and warm bread odors filled the air. The first things that the trio noticed, however, were the plants. Houseplants had overgrown their holders, spilling green waterfalls onto the floors. Flowers in vases were showing new growth, and the young Irish girl with blonde hair, freckles, and an amply filled low-cut green top was smiling at their entry. She wore a red bloom in her hair that was dripping nectar into the golden field below.

"Welcome to Gracie's!" The clerk was bright and chipper "We're having a special on triple layer chocolate cakes this week, so let me know if you see anything you like." She looked Edison up and down as she spoke, finishing with a wink.

Edison nodded, then leaned into Oreth. "Is it her?"

Oreth bit his lower lip, breathed in deeply, then shook his head. "I don't know. She's here, somewhere, but there's so much of her Nature that I can't pinpoint her."

Liara nodded, then pointed at the clerk.

"Well, I'll go talk with her, see if she knows anything."

"Wait." Edison paused. "Are you sure I shouldn't? I mean...umm...do you even speak Irish? I do, it wouldn't be any trouble," He finished with a half-smirk.

Liara gave him a tight-lipped smile. "No, Edison, that's all right; I think I can manage. You go work with Oreth – I'll handle her."

Edison turned to Oreth, grinning. "So, boss, what next?"

"Don't call me 'boss'." Oreth's eyes were moving, taking in the subtle differences in the environment. "I'll head upstairs; you scout out the grounds in case the clerk doesn't pan out. She's here somewhere," he repeated, "and she can't be *that* well hidden."

"Roger that." Edison gave Oreth a mock, two-finger salute. He turned to browse the pastries, listening to the conversation with one ear.

It almost made him laugh.

"Are you the Matron?"

"The what?"

"Holder of the Nature of Life?"

"Umm..is this a joke? Are we on T.V.?" The clerk glanced around, searching for a hidden camera, then coming back to Liara. "Look, I don't want to be rude, but if you're not buying anything, I'd appreciate if you..."

Her eyes fell on Liara's shoes – boots forged with fur inside, gold filigree outside, and as flexible as soft leather – and squealed.

"Oh my god!" The clerk's sudden exclamation caused Liara to jump. "Where did you get those? Online?" She came around the counter to get a better look. "Wow...I've never seen anything like these." She ran a finger over the tiny metal scales. "How much were they?" A glance at Liara's face, a flush in her own. "I mean, if that's not too personal."

Liara's face went red with pleasure, and her voice evinced obvious pride as she said, "I made them."

"No...way." The clerk just couldn't keep her hands off the boots, marveling at the texture and appearance. Liara looked at Edison, mouthing *help me.*

Edison waved good-bye, still smiling, and headed out the back of the shop. There was a small garden space here, with lilacs, roses, ferns, and all manner of flora woven together to form color pictures of animals: lions, buffalo, dolphins, and scorpions seemed to swim and crawl through this pocket of green.

He had to search for his breath. For several seconds, the power of the place held him in its grip, and he could not pull his eyes from the wonder.

"G'mornin, son." A strong woman's voice came from behind one of the pomegranate trees.

Edison turned to see a completely unremarkable woman coming around the trunk. She wore gardener's clothes – gloves, boots, mud-splattered apron – and her sun-browned, crinkled face held sparkling grey eyes behind her glasses. Her hair had been a fiery red once, but had dulled with age, and time had sprinkled it with snow.

"I'm sorry, ma'am; I didn't mean to bother you." He pointed at the topiaries – eagles flying in a green and yellow sky made from buttercups – and asked, "Did you make these?"

She tipped her head up, following Edison's eyes as he looked at the bushes. "Yes, these are my babies; hard work, you know, keeping them looking this way."

Edison nodded, face toward the eagle topiary but studying the woman out of the corner of his eye. "How did you get them to look so lifelike? It's incredible." He leaned in closer, and his voice dropped in awe. "Looks like they grew this way...I don't see any clipper marks or anything."

The woman's smile vanished like a mirage, and her eyes hardened. "Why?" Her posture stiffened as Edison's head jerked back toward her. "Why do you want to know?"

Edison held his hands up before him. "I'm not trying to cause trouble. My friends and I are just looking for someone..." Out of his peripheral vision, Edison could see the shrubs and trees writhing, curling, extending.

The woman advanced on Edison. Her grey eyes seemed to roil like thunderclouds on the horizon, and Edison could hear a powerful *thrum*, like a heartbeat, pulsing out from her every step. "There's no one here for you to find. Go home before someone follows you! Go on!" She shooed him with her hands, caked with dirt that was home to sprouting seedlings, growing before Edison's astonished gaze. "We don't want you here! Get! Get!"

Edison was flabbergasted — he could not

get a word in edgewise, something which didn't happen often. He kept trying to respond, but she was forcing him back toward the doorway with her approach.

"But...I...wait, please!" There was a *thump* as he bumped the wood of the door.

"No 'buts'." The angry gardener was only two feet from him, and the heartbeat sound crashed in on him, threatening to overwhelm his senses. "You just get out of here! You don't know..."

She trailed off as the door opened. Oreth and Liara stood in the passageway. She stared at the three Essentials for several moments.

"Guys, I think..."

The gardener interrupted Edison as she pointed a quivering finger at Oreth."You. I know you. You died, then Life returned to you, but the darkness still taints you. Death is angry. Azrael is angry and he hunts you. He hunts you, doesn't he? And you wish to bring him here?"

"No." Oreth shook his head. "We wish to kill him. And, we think we know how

(*Your enemy is coming, Father*)

– but we'll need your help."

The Matron's eyes went wide. She looked at each of them in turn, saw the seriousness in their eyes. "You...you're crazy. She leveled a finger at Liara, and the young woman flinched. "Woman, caretaker of the Forge's flames, you truly think that your artifice can conquer one such as he, who unmakes with a thought? You could not save your own father from his death, and yet you think to conquer the Death of us all? And you, young warrior," she continued, moving her pointer to indicate Edison, "enslaved to the culture created by your own Nature, adrift in the sea of words; how will you stop Death, who transcends language, thought, conceptualization? You believe that you can turn his power aside with your games, your computers, your Internet?"

Her hair moving in a nonexistent wind and her eyes burning with the power of Life, the Matron rounded on Oreth. "And you. Death claimed you once, master of Cities, and you have returned from his hold. Isn't that enough? Must you contend with an invincible adversary? Are you *that* foolish?"

"He's not invincible." Edison shook his head.

"He can't die, fool! He *is* Death. How can you kill him? How can you even inconvenience him?" She started pacing, waving her hands in the air as she spoke, her pulled-up bun continuing to unravel as more seedlings started pushing their way through the greying red.

"We know that he can be made vulnerable." Liara was speaking through the tears which had threatened to emerge. "We have seen him injured, injured him ourselves. He has weaknesses, just as everyone does!" The Matron sneered, her eyes falling on the smith with a mixture of pity and anger. Then she froze.

"If you have already fought him..." The Matron paused, her face paling. "He must already know – he will not let you rest, not if you know any weakness, any vulnerability. Yes? Yes. He'll come for you, you know that, don't you?"

"Matron. Yes, he might come for us. He was injured, but I know that a mere injury won't hold him for long. That's why we had to come see you." A sound wafted in from the distance on the salty sea breeze, noticeable only if one listened for it; it sounded like...screams?

"To bring Death here? Do you realize what you've done?" The Matron slapped Oreth across the face; the garden animals growled, howled, and roared in their turns. "Don't you realize that I'm the one he really wants?" Open shock registered on the faces of the three Essentials. "All the others, you're just delays – something to keep the power from bleeding out of him for a while." She laughed, an insane sound that went on too long.

"If he gets me and my Nature, though, he owns *everything*, the whole cycle. Life would serve Death, and this whole planet would die...but slowly, over millions of years. EVERYTHING." She spread her hands wide as she continued to laugh. "He doesn't even realize it!" She started to cry. "Or maybe he doesn't care. He just thinks that it's just a 'problem' he needs to solve."

"All the more reason for us to act *together*." Oreth stepped forward. "I told you, we have a plan that will help us defeat him, but you're part of it. You need to be *with* us."

"Grandma?" It was the clerk. "I'm not feeling so well. Can I close up early?"

"Sure, dear. Go on up to..." The Matron's eyes narrowed. "Rosy's *never* sick."

Everyone else was silent.

They heard the door open, and Rosy's voice saying, "I'm sorry, we're...clo...s..." and a loud thump as something hit the floor.

"He's here!" Liara spun around, summoning Harendar.

"No!" The plants broke their animal shapes and barricaded themselves against the door, vines burrowing into the wood and stone.

Edison started forward. "What about the girl?"

Oreth grabbed his arm. "She's dead, Edison! We need to figure out what *we're* going to do!"

The Matron rounded on Oreth. "He killed her, he killed her, it's your fault..." She started slamming her fists against Oreth's chest, and some of the seedlings on her head fell to the earth. "You bastard..."

The leaves on the edges of the barricade began to brown and wither.

"Matron!" Oreth grabbed her by her shoulders, held her up to look into his eyes. "You need to make him mortal!"

She looked at Oreth like he had grown a new eye in his forehead. "What the hell are you talking about?"

"Everything that's alive can die, Matron." Edison's eyes danced from her to the door as he spoke. "If he's alive, he can die, we can kill him — you need to remind the universe of that! *Make* him vulnerable! He's alive!"

"Well, if she's going to do it, she'd better hurry!" Liara tightened her grip, watching the increasing decay as it spread through the fortification.

"But...I..." Panic was evident in her voice.

"We're out of time!" Edison took a step back as the last of the branches rotted away, revealing the pitted, spongy wood of the decayed door behind.

The three Essentials took up combat positions around the Matron, Liara taking point, activating her wards and holding Harendar high; Edison and Oreth were next, each prepared with his own powers...powers which, they knew, were futile against Azrael.

The door collapsed on its own weight, leaving a ragged border of wood on the frame. Across the threshold stood the flame-scarred form of Azrael. His once-handsome face was a ruin, resembling a topographic map more than a man. His suit was immaculate, but his hands were frozen in near-claws.

"Hello, Oreth." The creature's resonant voice belied its mangled form. "I'm glad to see you alive." The scabrous eyes scanned the assembled group, noting their weapons and aggressive stances. "Does this really need to turn violent?" A bleeding, oozing hand gestured to the withering plants beside him. "I just want to be able to enjoy a garden without it collapsing around me, to watch children play without hearts bursting. I have not felt another's loving touch in *seven thousand years*," he said. "Have I not paid? These wounds Eriana inflicted are beyond even my power to heal – I still burn from her vengeance. Have I not paid enough? Can I not also be happy?"

"What you are asking isn't the problem." Oreth cut the air in front of him with his hand. "It's that you don't care about the consequences, the effects on humanity, who will die in order to give you this happiness."

"No one who wouldn't die anyway!" Azrael's teeth were black as his flesh. "You think that the mere 75-, 80-year lifespan of a human being means anything to me? That a civilization might fall in 300 years instead of 400?"

He laughed-- a terrible sight coming from his monstrous face.

"You beast!" The Matron strode forward, stepping out from behind Liara, her eyes red with tears. "You monster! How...how dare you! You do not have the right, not here, not in my sanctuary!"

Azrael's eyes widened with a sound like the crushing of an insect's chitinous shell. "Is...is it you?"

The Matron's tears struck the ground, and overgrowth burst from the site, knocking Liara, Oreth, and Edison away and lunging for Azrael.

The vines and thorns wrapped around Azrael's form, collapsing around him like a caterpillar's cocoon. Oreth stood up.

"Why aren't we feeling his aura? Why aren't we weakening?" Liara asked as she regained her feet.

The foliage covering the burned Essential began to brown, curling up and crisping. "It doesn't matter!" said Edison. "We need to get the hell out of here." Vines snapped. "Now!"

"No!" Oreth braced himself. "We brought him here; I'm not running again." He looked to his fellows. "Matron, we need your help, and we can end this here and now. Stand with us. Be brave."

The Matron's hands shook as she watched Azrael breaking free of his prison like an escaping butterfly. Her eyes glistened with tears, and her voice trembled, but she said, "All right. I'll try."

Azrael stood, casting off the last remnants of greenery as he appraised his adversaries. His gaze passed over each, searching, probing, and settled on Oreth.

"You plan to raise your hand against me, old friend?"

Oreth nodded. "You've been bearing this burden too long, Azrael. Give it up. Let the Nature pass to another."

Azrael laughed, long and deep. "Another? There are no others, Oreth! No one else can withstand Death's power; it almost overwhelms *me*. If that power passed to one of the brainless cattle walking the Earth, imagine the devastation!" Azrael walked toward the group, his footsteps burning trails in the grass.

"You call me murderous, say that I don't care for the deaths I cause, yet you demand I do something that will likely end billions of human lives, animals, lay waste to millions of hectares of forests and grasslands. Massacre entire food chains, entire ecosystems. And this assumes that my successor could even rein in the power at all; the damage could be much higher." He shook his head, the crisp flesh at his neck crackling with his movement. "You should really think about these things, Oreth."

Liara hitched up her grip on her hammer. "Did those things happen when the Nature came to you, Azrael?"

Azrael stopped, his face falling, his gaze down for a moment.

"No. Not then." His voice was weak, uncertain. Then he picked up his head and regained his focus. "The gift, the curse, was passed to me. Death chose *me*, no others."

"NOW!" Edison, having waited until his foe seemed most distracted, dived at Azrael as the Matron sank to her knees. She drove her hands into the dirt, plant roots lacing into her fingers, piercing skin.

Azrael's hand came up, his fingers outstretched as he sought to block Edison's path, to drain the momentum from his leap and bring him down. The dark, necrotic energy rippled down his arm, shimmering like a heat-haze, and leapt from his fingertips.

The force was met by an undulating tide of green, lush and verdant, screaming from the Earth as it interposed itself between Azrael and Edison, whose leap carried him over the collision of powers to land on his enemy, knocking the both of them to the ground.

Azrael's control of his power wavered as he sought to free himself from Edison, wrapping his fingers around the godling's neck; the emerald energy broke through and cascaded over him. His eyes widened.

It was as if two planets had collided. The Essentials recoiled from the battle being waged between the two Natures of Life and Death in Azrael's soul, Azrael asserting his right to command Death, to repudiate and deny it, while Life demanded his return to the natural cycle, to feed his materials, spiritual and otherwise, to the future generations as was right.

Azrael's fingers went slack as all of his attention diverted to this struggle, the conflict distorting the air around him, causing him to appear hazy and unreal.

Liara charged as Edison rolled away,

coughing. She brought Harendar's flaming bulk down on Azrael's head, the impact tremor shattering the windows of the shop and driving his body into the ground. Oreth clenched his fists and *WATERFORD* responded, light poles uprooting and twisting themselves around their enemy, lashing him to the ground and weighing him down; bricks from the walk melted over him, entombing his lower half as Liara's blows continued to strike home.

Edison glanced toward the Matron, and his breath caught. She was surrounded in the same verdant aura which had interposed itself between Azrael and Edison, but she appeared to be in the throes of a seizure; her eyes had rolled into the back of her head, her nose and ears were bleeding, grass roots had dug into her entrenched fingers and were burrowing up her arms. He ran to her.

"Hold on, hold on." She didn't respond, but he kept speaking. "Don't let go, you're okay, you're doing it."

Edison could hear the crunching of bones and pounding of metal against flesh behind him, but his focus was on keeping the Matron in the game. His spirits rose as he saw her pupils roll forward and focus on his face. Her mouth worked.

"I'm sorry." Her eyes were beginning to bleed. "I...I can't..." Her eyelids covered the blood-soaked orbs as she slipped into unconsciousness.

Oreth watched as Liara hammered at Azrael, pulping his skin and muscle and splintering bone. The Essential of Death was still alive, he knew, because he could still feel the intense struggle, the battle between two fundamental forces of reality, being waged.

Then Oreth saw Death. The robed, skeletal form drifted toward the site of Azrael's entombment, fingers outstretched. There was only one medallion on its hand now – Oreth's – and Oreth could sense an emotion

(*joy*)

coming from the figure.

He allowed himself a moment of exultation, of hope...and then he saw the grass. Like the explosion of an atomic bomb, the grass died in an ever-expanding circle from Azrael's position. The Death-figure recoiled, a new chain materializing as it vanished once more.

Liara stopped in mid swing, her muscles

straining. Harendar's flames flickered and sputtered, dimming to a candle's intensity. The great hammer dropped from her fingers as she collapsed to the ground, beginning to cry as her muscles failed her.

The power of Azrael's aura struck Oreth, then, and Edison; it was as if they had been hollowed out, pitted. They were only shells with no magic, no strength – only fatigue and pain. The metal streetlight and brick walk rotted, rusted, shattered, and Azrael rose, his flesh and bone knitting as he, once again, denied his own Death.

"ENOUGH!" Azrael's voice drained any remaining strength from his opponents. His power washed over them, rolling like waves of surf, pounding at their selfhood, their consciousness, their lives.

"I am *done* with this." He brushed himself off as the last wounds closed on his face. Oreth struggled to stand, to move, but could only raise his head, and that felt like moving a mountain. Azrael's footfalls echoed in the empty caverns of the Essentials' minds.

He gestured toward the prone Matron. "I am going to take her with me. I am going to take her Nature and subordinate it to my own. I am going to be able to walk the Earth, enjoy trees, make love." He sighed and bent down to Oreth's face, and kissed his forehead.

Oreth suppressed his scream.

"I'm sorry, old friend, but I don't need you anymore. You can be thankful for that, I suppose, but don't worry – I'm not going to kill you. Not today, and, if you leave me be, not ever." Azrael rose. "Enjoy your immortality, Oreth, and know that I am still your friend."

Taking the Matron's limp form into his arms, Azrael spoke a brief incantation, then dissipated into a black mist, thinning and vanishing into the air.

His departure felt like rolling a boulder off of the immortals' chests – their energy returned as if it had never left, and they helped one another to their feet, none daring to look the others in the eye. The sounds of fire trucks and ambulances reached their ears.

Oreth spoke first. "We should go." Liara nodded, and Edison kicked at the ground.

"Yeah, I guess."

Oreth put one hand on each of their shoulders, and pulled back toward New York.

They vanished just as the first of the emergency personnel hit the scene, leaving behind the devastated topiary garden.

19 – DANCING TO DEATH'S DIRGE

The three Essentials had taken up their seats at their customary Denny's, Oreth across from the others, coffees all around. The waiters had changed shifts three times since they had arrived. No one had spoken yet.

They sat in silence for a long, long time, sipping caffeine and glancing out the window and at each other.

The server came by, refilled their coffees, left.

Oreth opened his mouth. Closed it. Sighed. Drank more coffee.

The sun began to come up again, the second sunrise they had seen while in these seats.

The three looked at each other once more, then:

"What the hell was that?"

"What the fuck happened?"

"How did he do that?"

Edison, Oreth, and Liara blinked, then started giggling. The giggles progressed to chuckles, and then to laughter, then to rolling on the floor, tears pouring as Edison's water glass fell on the floor and shattered. Men, women, and children in booths around the restaurant stood up to marvel at the unfolding scene of hilarity; the laughter sounded *wrong* to them, not the laughter of joy, or humor, but of madness. It was the laughter of those who *must* laugh, who can do *nothing* else, because if they do...

The server ran back over, his eyes full of concern as he watched the three demigods trapped in the throes of their own laughter.

"Sirs? Ma'am? Is everything all right?" The teenaged boy looked back and forth, from one to the other of them. "I'll...I'll go get the manager."

"No." Edison was still laughing, struggling to his feet and taking deep breaths to control himself. "No...we're okay. My friend just told us a damn funny joke." He clapped the waiter on the shoulder, then glanced down at the name-tag on his red vest as he pulled out a hundred-dollar bill. "Here, Sam. On me. Sorry about the water glass." Edison smiled. The others had composed themselves by now, large grins splitting their faces.

"Th..thanks! Thank you very much!" Sam almost knocked over another server as he backed away from the table. He turned and rushed to the headwaiter, saying something about being let off early. Oreth shook his head, then beckoned for Edison to sit back down with them.

"Look." Oreth interlaced his fingers, tapping the index ones together. "We need some time to figure out what to do next. I'm going to try and come up with a plan. You two need to do some footwork. Investigate, try to dig up rumors about any weaknesses he might have, maybe call in some favors, get friends behind you who don't necessarily like the idea of Azrael bleeding the world to death."

Edison's smile faltered. "What *can* we do, Oreth? He beat us. We lost. There's no way to stop him now."

Oreth shook his head. "Talk like that and you'll be your own prophet, Pheidippides." The use of his old name caused Edison's head to snap up and his eyes to narrow as Oreth continued. "Azrael's not the only one who's been around a long time, you know."

Liara nodded. "All right, why don't we meet up at the Motel 6 where you found me? Same room. We can check it out, see if Azrael left anything behind. All right, Edison?"

Edison stood, helped Liara to her feet, then linked arms with her as he affected a British accent. "Well, then, madam, shall we away?" The two snickered, their laughter trailing after them as they headed to the nearby bus stop.

Oreth watched them leave, shaking his head.

I remember that. So long ago, but I remember it. He sighed and blinked back tears. *Eriana. I'm sorry.*

He shook his head, then transported himself to Central Park. The city welcomed him there, cool breezes caressing him and pleasant aromas surrounding him. Oreth closed his eyes, trying to clear his mind, to meditate on a solution, a possible response.

It was lost to him. Despite his bravado and confidence in front of his comrades, he had no idea how they were going to succeed.

I don't know what to do. I don't even know if there is something I can do.

Oreth hung his head in despair, eyes still closed, tears leaking out. The sound of the sprinklers watering the grass intruded upon his consciousness, which was then interrupted itself by

(*Don't give up*)

a thought that was not his own. He wiped his eyes.

Was that my imagination?

(*No there is a way but I need your help*)

Oreth blinked. That was no random thought, but a directed communication. He put his hands over his ears to block out other sounds.

Who are you?

(*I am everyone – we were here and now*

we're gone but I remain. There is an imbalance and it must be corrected. You must help me)

Why are you speaking to me?

(I am within you my physical my body is yours)

Oreth considered. What could that mean? His eyes widened as a possible explanation occurred to him, and his hand flattened over his chest.

Are you...the Egg? The Alabaster Egg?

(The destruction, the death of the universe is at hand. We can stop it. I can show you how)

How do I know I can trust you?

(Do you have a choice?)

After a moment's consideration, Oreth nodded, then closed his hands together and submitted himself to the tutelage of the ancient relic, repository for untold power.

No one around him ever noticed.

~~~

Liara swiped the electronic key for room 224 at the Motel 6. The light beeped green and
~~~

the lock clicked open.

She suppressed a shudder as she stepped into the room. The room had been cleaned, of course – sheets changed, air freshened, towels replaced – but the energy, the memory, was still here. A brief image of looking up at Azrael's face as he touched her seared her mind.

"You okay?" Edison was waiting behind her. Liara realized that she had stopped in the doorway. She went all the way inside, allowing Edison to enter and the door to close.

"Let's look around." She blinked as Edison flicked on the light. "Maybe there's something we can find, sense, that will help us."

"Yeah. Maybe we'll come across the *Analysis of a Death-God* issue of Cosmo – twelve things they wish we didn't know!"

Liara slapped his shoulder. "Keep the smart-assery to yourself. I'll look under the beds; you check the drawers and closets."

Liara could feel the residue of Azrael's presence, almost a smell, like it was sunk deep into the wood and brick of the room.

"Liara?" Edison's voice was coming from the main closet.

"Yes? Did you find something?" She kept

searching under the bed.

Edison was quiet, and Liara came up to look at him. He was gazing at her, his face torn.

"What is it?"

"We haven't had much of a chance to talk lately, what with resurrecting Oreth and getting the Matron captured and all, but there was something I wanted to ask you."

"What?"

"Did...did you mean what you said?" He rubbed his hands together and glanced back and forth.

"When?" She felt her heart beginning to pick up speed.

"We...we haven't had the chance to talk about it...when Azrael had us after I dropped the Egg, you know?" He kept stammering, almost repeating himself, visibly trying to keep his tongue from flapping in his nervousness.

"Oh." Liara's face had flushed, and her throat had begun to close up. "What...what were you asking?"

Edison took two steps toward her. "Did you mean it?"

The moment dragged out for a long time. Edison's hopeful eyes began to dim as they were confronted by Liara's silence.

"I guess n..."

"Yes!" The single word burst out from her lips. Edison's head snapped up, his eyes narrowed.

"Yes?"

"Yes, I meant it, Edison." Liara stood, began to pace around the room. "I meant it, Edison, I really did." She refused to meet his eyes, and her speech matched her pacing.

"Because I did too."

She stopped in her tracks.

"I..." He glanced away, swallowed, turned back, tried again. "I...I've been falling for you for a while now, Liara. You're brave, clever, and kick serious ass." Edison laughed and Liara smiled, her blush darkening.

"Flattery, flattery." She glanced at the ground. "Why are you bringing this up now? We have things...we're supposed to find something out...for Oreth..."

Edison had stepped up to her and covered her lips with his. For a moment, her body stiffened in surprise, but then she softened, their tentative kiss becoming passionate probing; their hands wrapped around each other's backs, as lust burned away the fear and doubt Liara had carried around since seeing Oreth in that hospital.

They separated, still in each other's arms, their breathing heavy. Their eyes searched, looking for confirmation, acknowledgement of the heat which had been simmering in their hearts. It was there.

Fingers could not move fast enough to reveal more skin for lips to caress; Liara laughed as Edison struggled to find a way to remove her buttonless blouse; her fingers traced a near-invisible pattern on the left sleeve, and the woven metal dissolved into the Otherspace, revealing her upper half to his hungry eyes and questing hands.

Liara sighed as the two of them fell onto the bed, Edison's tongue and teeth finding her nipples, teasing, then suckling her soft flesh as if he was dying of thirst. Her fingers roamed his back, nails leaving thin paths of red skin over his muscles. She grasped his shoulders and pulled him back up to her face for another kiss, pressing her breasts into his chest and feeling their warmth pooling.

"Are you..." She silenced him, putting a finger to his lips and smiling with her own. A soft kiss followed by a "yes," and there was no more conversation, only the irrepressible vocalizations of love made physical.

Their joining was swift, yet Liara felt their souls seal together as their bodies did, a seamless join between two metals on a forge, one made from two and stronger for it, something that she had never felt with Oreth in times past. Conscious thought was but a memory as their lovemaking changed from the slow, measured pace of the forge to the wild frenzy of a jackhammer; faster and faster their bodies collided, speeding toward the ultimate end – a perfect union of flesh, soul, and heart.

That end, when it came, was hotter and more furious than the heart of the Sun. Liara's scream as she climaxed reverberated through the room on several levels, driving out the remaining Death taint. Life had returned, in all its wet, warm, and salty magnificence.

The two collapsed against each other, the fires of passion now banked, each looking into the loving eyes looking back. Edison smiled.

"Damn.".

Liara laughed; it was the happiest she had

felt in a long, long time. "Damn."

"We're supposed to be trying to track down others, finding a way to stop Azrael," he said.

Liara snuggled closer to Edison. "No hurry."

"No hurry."

20 – TWO SIDES OF DEATH'S COIN

Exactly one hour, seventeen minutes, thirty-two seconds after the conversation had begun, Oreth regained his senses. When he opened his eyes, the first things he saw were the pigeons that had chosen his inert form as a roost, and the New Yorkers surrounding him who cheered as he moved to shake them off, walking away, laughing to themselves and each other.

The Egg was not an especially effective

teacher. Still, the idea it had presented had merit, had possibilities.

And, as the thing had so eloquently stated, Oreth really had no other choice. *Something* had to be done, and done now before the damage got worse. Already he could feel the change begotten by Azrael's subjugation of the Matron; the small but definite increase in murder, suicide, death by disease...all these causes and more, perhaps a half percent increase all told, but over seven billion people...

"Do you have any change, sir?"

Oreth turned his head; a woman, shabby clothes, and with deep bruises under her eyes was standing a few feet away; gaze averted, hand outstretched, hope, fear, and shame warring in her face . Three children were sleeping under a bush nearby.

Oreth stood, paralyzed by the coincidence. *Could* it be coincidence, given what he now knew? He held his hand over his chest and wondered.

"Sir?"

"I'm sorry." He flashed a bright smile. "I don't have any change, but I have something better." He reached his hand toward her forehead. She recoiled.

"Please." His word stopped her flight. She met his gaze and froze, held captive by his soul. He touched her brow.

<<Fateful fortune favors few –
Given gifts most never knew
Suffering brings you great reward,
Greater than a golden hoard.>>

A soft blue light sank into her head, dissipating and vanishing from view. The ragged woman shook her head, her eyes clearing, flicking over Oreth's face.

"Don't give up." He took a step back. "Good things are coming your way."

"I...I believe you. She was staring after him in wide-eyed wonder as he walked away, disappearing behind a tree.

And reappearing outside Room 224, Oreth opened the door into the room.

"I've got a couple..." His voice was interrupted by a girlish scream and the sound of fumbling fingers clutching at fabric as blankets were pulled up to chins. The wide eyes of Liara and Edison peered at Oreth from beet-red faces.

Should have known. Oreth shook his head,

holding back his laughter. *It's about time.*

"...of ideas." He stopped shaking his head and smiled. "I'm guessing you two haven't found anything out?" He paused. "About Azrael, I mean."

"Umm..." Liara's eyes were trying their best to avoid his.

"Unfortunately not." Edison gave Oreth a thumbs-up. "But we had the utmost faith in you, good buddy. We knew you'd manage something."

Oreth smiled, spread his hands, and bowed. "Glad that I didn't disappoint. Now, if you two don't mind getting dressed, I'm going to call Rob; we have somewhere to go."

"Where are we headed?" Liara gestured, and her garments began to rematerialize.

"Golgotha."

~~~

"So, why are we going to Golgotha?" Edison's voice was raised; he was speaking to be heard over the raucous strains of Nirvana's *Smells Like Teen Spirit.*

"I need to speak to Death."
~~~

Liara spoke up. "Umm...I'm sure that Azrael told you *not* to come talking to him, or he would kill you."

"Not Azrael. Death itself. I've seen it. I should be able to talk to it. Convince it to help us."

"Wait." Edison waved his hands in a *hold on a sec* gesture. "You're saying that Death is...what, the Grim Reaper? Seriously?"

Oreth did not respond; he simply looked at Edison until the younger Essential nodded and whistled. "Seriously."

"Isn't that...risky?" Harendar appeared in Liara's hand. "What if Death won't cooperate?"

"A possible danger." Oreth nodded his head. "But I think that Edison here had the answer. He told both of us, but neither of us listened, did we, Edison?"

Edison's face was blank for a few moments, then his eyes lit up. "A bet? A game?"

Oreth nodded.

"You're going to bet with Death? What do you have? What's your wager?"

Oreth smiled. "Something worthwhile. Don't worry," he added, seeing Liara's eyes narrow. "I'm not planning to wager my life or my soul. Trust me on the rest of it, okay?"

Reluctant nods from the assembled personages. "What do we do, then?" Liara released her grip on her hammer, and it returned to the Otherspace. "I can tell you don't want us with you when you talk to this Death-thing."

"You two need to go confront Azrael." There was a sharp intake of breath. "If Azrael has done what he planned, linked to the Matron's Nature – and he has, believe me – then he shouldn't be radiating that death-aura of his. Talk to him. Stall him. When – and if – my plan works, take him out." Oreth leaned forward, sweat glistening on his brow. "Do not, I repeat, *do not* attack him if you don't see something. I don't know what it'll look like – light, maybe, or just a feeling or something – but if you don't get that sensation, *back off*." He sighed. "No point in getting you two killed if my plan doesn't work."

"This sounds like a terrible plan." The two men turned toward Liara. "I mean, on the off chance that you *can* negotiate with this death-spirit, then you have to win your wager, *then* there has to be some sort of tangible evidence that you have done so, and *then* we have to be able to take Azrael down." She held up her fingers. "That's four, count them, *four* nearly impossible things that *all* have to go right. Is this really the best we have? The best we can come up with?"

Oreth considered this, tapping his finger to his chin. "Um...yes. It's the best I've got, anyway – and, if I recall, I was the only one actually working on solutions."

Heat filled Liara's cheeks. "Oh, right. Sorry."

Oreth waved her comment away. "Liara, I think this will work. Our direct approach ended up biting us in the ass; at least this way, Azrael probably won't be so pissed at you if it doesn't work out – you can just walk away, live your lives." He looked out the window, watching the landscape go by.

"Honestly, I wouldn't be surprised if you didn't want to come. It's a lot harder to risk your life when you have something to live for." He turned his head back to his friends. "But I *can't* do this without you. And it needs to be done."

Edison called out, "Maestro! We need a change of tune!"

"What's your poison?" Nirvana went quiet.

"You got any Journey?"

Rob rolled his eyes in the mirror, and his head swayed back and forth as he spoke. "No, why would I have Journey? I'd have to like rock-and-roll or something to listen to Journey."

"Smartass." Edison flipped him the bird. "Give us *Any Way You Want It*, if you don't mind."

He turned back to the others as the music started to play, face deadpan. "Shit just got real."

~~~

It was done. By whatever Gods may exist, it was done.

Azrael reached out to the fig tree, marveling as the leaves did not crumble, as the fruit remained stubbornly whole, fresh, and, as he determined when he bit into it, delicious.

Visitors and citizens in the city of Jerusalem passed by this white-suited figure with barely a glance – much to Azrael's delight, there was a decided scarcity of spontaneous
~~~

cases of stage-four colorectal cancer, or catastrophic strokes, or heart explosions. In fact, not a single person died while walking down the sidewalk Azrael stood on.

He breathed in once, twice--deep, lingering breaths. Little things like this, the brush of others in a crowded space, or the simple lack of terror surrounding his existence, are what made everything worthwhile. For once, he did not need to cloak himself in the *Nizra'el* for fear that his presence, and its side effects, would cause an attack against him and force him to slaughter yet more. Instead, he was able to revel in the conversations being held around him, luxuriate in the petty greetings given by the men and women he passed.

Azrael thought back to Oreth's eyes as he had lain on the ground in defeat. For a moment, his heart was heavy; Oreth had been one of the few who, although terrified by the eldest Essential, had been willing to talk to and work with him. It hurt to humiliate his old friend that way. It did.

At least it doesn't really matter now. It's done. I hope he understands someday, and we can be friends again.

He shrugged to himself. *Perhaps not, and then I hope I am not forced to kill him.*

Two streets over, a three-and-a-half month old child died of SIDS. He should not have.

Azrael did not care.

21 – GOLGOTHA, HILL OF DEATH

Oreth stood on the site where Christ died.

This was not the place where others had built a temple and memorial; Oreth was on a hill to the north of the Lion's Gate, outside Jerusalem's walls. Christ had been crucified here more than 350 years before Oreth had fallen at the Visigoth's sack of Rome, and still the energy of that act permeated the very stone.

I don't know if he was the son of God, but he was sure somebody.

Security had tried to stop him, of course – given the new tensions between Israel, Iran, and Syria, any Arabic-looking gentleman without proper identification was bound to be detained – but Oreth had "convinced" them to look elsewhere.

Edison would have been disappointed in me, he realized. *No Star Wars reference.*

If the stories were true about Jesus, then he and Oreth had one thing in common. They had both come back from the dead.

Maybe that was enough, here.

Oreth prepared his ritual space, using the knowledge gleaned from his communion with the artifact pulsing in his chest. He carved sigils and symbols into the dirt, the amalgams of thousands of religions over thousands of years, none with any inherent power but all backed by the will of the user. Ancient spells, ancient tongues, and ancient runes, all beckoning, summoning, conjuring one thing, something Oreth had believed nonexistent until recently.

Death Itself.

Oreth's incantations began.

~~~
~~~

Edison and Liara disembarked from Rob's bus; Edison handed the driver a folded note. "Oreth said to give this to you." He clapped Rob on the shoulder again. "Good luck, and thanks for everything."

"You too." Rob stood. "I still don't really know what the hell you guys are or what's going on, but I haven't felt this much a part of something important since my college days." He put his hand out, and Edison took it. "Give 'em hell, my man."

"We'll do that." Edison grinned, stepping down the stairwell of the bus.

His smile disappeared along with their ride.

"Edison...what the hell are we doing?" Liara's eyes burrowing into his. "We know we can't beat him."

Edison nodded and hugged her close. "You're right." His breath tickled her ear. "It'll take a miracle." He held her out at arm's length. He smiled. "Then again, aren't we miracle workers?"

"This is serious, Edison." Liara was struggling to keep the corners of her mouth from upturning. "What are we going to *do*?"

"Do you trust Oreth?"

"What? Well...yes...I guess..."

"Yes or no."

Liara thought, thought back to when Oreth's life had been burning with her own like a fetus suckling the warmth of its mother.

How he had charged in and confronted a god for the sake of a woman he didn't know.

How *she* had already risked her life for his.

"Yes." She nodded. "I do."

"So do I." Edison grasped her hand, held it tight. "More than I ever did, even when I was new. So if he says to be ready, that he has it under control, I choose to believe him." He grinned again. "It's better than the alternative of having no plan and no hope, right?"

Liara nodded. "All right. I just wish I knew more about this plan of his."

"Well, me too." He gestured at the city scenery around him. "At least he sent us some-where with historical merit." He laughed. "Jerusalem! City of God and all that, you know!"

Liara pointed to the arched windows and wooden walls which held lights illuminating the words *Shababeek Restaurant.* "He's in there?"

"Oreth said that the bus would take us where we needed to be." Edison shrugged. "And, being that it took us here..."

"It could have meant across the street." Liara pointed at the internet café across the way, filled with teens and twenty-somethings sipping coffee and using borrowed bandwidth.

They stared at each other for a moment, then laughed.

Edison took in the sight of the well-dressed patrons and breathed in the rich aromas from the storefront. "Hope we don't need reservations."

~~~

The dark storm clouds were absent, Oreth noted as he finished the first set of incantations. Unfortunate.

Rituals should *always* have dark storm clouds involved.

Instead, the stars in the night sky twinkled, keeping vigil over the work he was doing. He tossed the match into the great rune signifying
~~~

the concept of *binding,* of *coercion.* The rune began to burn with a violet flame, tall and proud, reaching to the heavens, invisible to men but not to the angels, if such existed.

And not invisible to Azrael.

I hope that the others have him distracted. Oreth glanced over at the cityscape. *I don't need him interrupting.*

He began carving the second set of runes.

~~~

The parlor of Shababeek resembled the interior of every Middle-Eastern restaurant since Rick's Café – smoky, with dim orange lighting, arched ceilings, and balconies. Hundreds of patrons dined on fine Mediterranean foods; waiters delivered lamb, curry, flambé dishes, rice, or figs to hungry customers, and the smells of food competed with the sickly-sweet nargeela smoke. The maître-d, a Palestinian by the looks of him, small but radiating authority, addressed the two Essentials.

"Can I help you?"

<<A friend is waiting for us,>> Edison replied in Arabic, causing a wave of relief to wash
~~~

over the other's face.

<<And your friend's name?>>

Liara stepped forward, and his attention moved to her. <<He's a black man, wearing an all-white suit.>> The maître-d's eyes lit up.

<<Ah! Yes!>> He pointed at a table in the center of the restaurant, where the very same being that had come so close to killing them on several occasions was sitting surrounded by piles of dishes, some empty, many not. His eyes were alight and the smile on his face evident as he shared a private joke with his waiter, a square of baklava in one hand and a lamb skewer with green peppers and onions in the other. The waiter laughed as he refilled Azrael's glass with a rich red wine.

<<He has been here for some time.>> The maître-d held his hands together and smiled. <<He hasn't slowed down, but he gave a generous payment in advance.>>

<<That's the way he does things,>> Edison struggled to keep his smile on. <<May we go see him?>>

The man hesitated a moment. <<I beg your pardon, but I would like to tell him you are here before you approach his table.>> Edison nodded.

Edison tapped Liara on the elbow. "Ten bucks says he starts killing people when he sees us."

"You're on."

The maître-d bent low over the table, speaking to Azrael and pointing toward the foyer where Liara and Edison stood. Azrael smiled and motioned for the two of them to come over.

"I win." Liara threaded her arm through Edison's.

"We'll see."

~~~

All the runes were lit – binding, beseechment, Death, agreement, power. The smokeless flames surrounding Oreth blocked his view of the city. He was working blind now.

Oreth drew a silver knife and made an incision up his arm. The blood dripped into a pentacle, inscribed with its points linking the burning runes.

<<I have escaped you once,>> His words rippled the air around him, like heat-haze on a
~~~

summertime highway. <<My blood should be cold in my veins, yet your hand has not closed on me. We have unfinished business, you and I.>> He raised his hands to the heavens. <<I invoke thee, Thanatos, Grim Reaper, Rider of the Pale Horse. Appear.>>

The blood on the ground began to move upward, defying gravity as it flowed, coating a cloak or robe, folds of cloth dyed crimson running down to outstretched skeletal hands, and up to the hood and skull of Death.

Oreth knelt before it.

~~~

"Come! Sit!" Azrael's voice was muffled, his mouth still full of rice. Liara and Edison pulled up chairs as the maître-d asked them if they needed anything.

Edison handed the man a fifty-dollar bill. <<No, I think he's got plenty here for all of us,>>

Azrael swallowed his mouthful, chasing it down with a glass of watermelon juice. "To what do I owe the pleasure?" Without waiting, he turned his head to Liara. "And you, it's good
~~~

to see you without that hammer coming at my skull."

Liara smiled. "I'm sure. It's nice to be able to hold my head up in your presence as well."

"Isn't it though?" He laughed, a rich sound. "The power's still there, no doubt about that, but I don't have to worry about my waiter's eyeballs dissolving into his head."

"Nice image." Edison grimaced, then picked up a glass of water.

"That's what I had to live with." Azrael put his fork down, his smile disappearing. "I'm sorry that we had to...forcibly...disagree, but I hope you can understand."

Azrael raised his arms, encompassing the whole of the restaurant within them.

"For millennia, even you, my peers, have considered me a monster. Inhuman. Well, let me ask you: how, exactly, is one supposed to be human when he can't eat, drink, or make merry? How long would you last, how long would you stay yourselves with no real connection to anyone?" He shook his head.

"Is the Matron still alive, Azrael?" Liara began chewing on a piece of bread.

"No." He shook his head. "I couldn't risk

what happened with Despoina happening again." Azrael drank another gulp of juice. "No, I'd rather someone new hold the Nature, so they don't question why it feels the way it does, or why it's tied to me."

Edison laughed. "Nice. Just let some poor bastard hitch their car to your train, huh? What if he doesn't like your terms?"

Azrael looked over at Edison, then shrugged. "Then I kill him."

Liara blinked. "What, just like that?"

"Yes, just like that." He took a sip of red wine, swished it in his mouth, swallowed. "I do hope it doesn't come to that, of course." He took a baklava square in his hand, studied it for a moment, then spoke again. "Contrary to popular belief, I don't actually *like* killing people." He took a bite of his square, the sweet crunching in his mouth.

"At least, most of the time." The crumbs of baklava sprayed from his lips.

Liara and Edison glanced at each other.

Azrael wiped his mouth on the napkin. "So why are you *really* here?" He turned his eyes from one to the other of his companions. "And why isn't Oreth with you?"

Edison shrugged. "He's pissed, honestly. He doesn't like to lose."

"Is he, now?" Azrael leaned back in his chair and started chewing on a toothpick.

Liara nodded. "Very. Not to mention scared. You threatened him pretty seriously back there, and he knows you have the muscle to back it up."

"Hmm." Azrael nodded, scratching at his chin and then sitting back up. "So, you two are here for, what? Peace talks?"

"No." Edison shook his head. "Actually, he wanted us to come find out about the Matron. I think he was hoping to convince her to renege, just like you were saying." Liara glanced at him, then nodded.

"We were supposed to find out where she was," she added. "Doesn't really matter, though, if she's dead."

Azrael laced his hands together on the table. "So, you're saying, basically, that the man who has spent tremendous effort on thwarting my plans, who has come very close to doing so on several occasions, and who has the benefit of the military and tactical knowledge of millennia of human experience, sent you two here to give away his plans while he sits at home crying to himself?" He laughed. "I don't think so."

His smile transformed into a scowl, and his power pulsed in his eyes.

"Here's what we're going to do." He waved his hand around the room. "The two of you are going to tell me what he's up to, or everyone in this restaurant is going to die."

Liara inhaled in shock.

"And if that doesn't convince you, then I'll genocide the city. Then the country."

"Are you...?" Edison's eyes were wide and his skin was pale.

Azrael's hand pistoned out, grabbing the front of Edison's shirt and hauling him over the table, sending dishes flying. A few customers stirred, glancing over to the center of the restaurant, but no one interfered.

"Am I what, Edison?" His breath still smelled of the spices he had consumed. "Serious? Yes. I am. I know Oreth, and he does not do *anything* without a deeper plan behind it – especially now that I know he has his memory restored to him."

Liara put a hand on Azrael's, which still

held Edison in its grip. "How did you know that?"

"You think you were the only one to know of the Egg?" Azrael's lips pressed together, forming a thin line. "If you had brought that to me, rather than wielding it as a weapon...but no matter. You must understand that the lives of a few dozen, few thousand, few *million* humans are irrelevant to me at this point. I have been present at, been *aware* of, the deaths of over one hundred billion souls." Azrael glared toward the maître-d, who was speaking to newly-arrived British guests, a family of five.

The maître-d put his hands on his abdomen, hunched over, and then screamed. The sound summoned other employees, and patrons dialed the police and emergency services on their phones. The stricken man's screams persisted, rising in pitch and volume until he lost consciousness a few moments later.

"Appendix burst." Azrael smiled at the shocked, appalled faces at his table. "So unfortunate."

Liara held her hand over her mouth; Edison's face was ghostly, and sweat had begun to flow from his forehead.

"Now, do we have an understanding?" Azrael took another sip of his wine. "What is my old friend up to?"

~~~

Oreth stood before the gruesome shape floating in the air. "You're rather an eloquent speaker, sir."

I am bound by your spells, but I also find your proposal acceptable, godling. The thoughts rolled from the figure like a boiling mist, tickling Oreth's mind.

"And my conditions?"

Also acceptable.

"So be it."

So be it.

Oreth took Death's hand. A small sigil appeared on the man's wrist, a sign of the agreement reached.

"Now, I just need to go find him, bring him here..." Oreth began to turn.

There is no need. He is already here.

~~~

Azrael stepped out of the night, holding both Liara and Edison by their necks. He tossed them aside, their bodies crumpling on the ground, semiconscious.

"Good evening, Oreth..." His words cut off when his eyes fell on the crimson-clad specter at Oreth's side, and the confident smile vanished from his face.

"You...you should not be here." He pointed at the apparition, his hand trembling.

I am bound to answer the summons, and to abide by the contracts created.

Oreth's smile was grim. "You aren't the only one who remembers ancient magics, 'old friend.'"

"What have you done?" Azrael's eyes remained on the figure, even as he took a step back.

"Only what I thought I had to do." Oreth sighed. "You're insane, Azrael. You are no longer human, no longer anything except a monster." Oreth leveled a finger at his adversary and continued, "You are no longer worthy to hold the power you possess. Surrender it and die as a man, or I will be forced to destroy you."

"Who are you to judge me?" Azrael snarled

as he walked, his words coming more like an angry dog than a man. "You abandoned the woman you loved, who loved you, to centuries of torment and anger. Your weakness led to the destruction of millions." Azrael returned Oreth's accusing gesture. "You are at least as liable for these deaths as I am!"

Oreth smiled, small and sad. "Yes, I am." He raised his head. "But that does not change what must be done, Azrael."

Azrael's eyes flicked back and forth between the two before him. He raised his hand toward the specter. "Begone!" He focused his power on Death, abjuring it, casting it away.

The force rippled, shattering stones and withering weeds. It slammed into the skeletal form, a wave smashing into a rock on the shore.

Like that rock, Death remained.

I am empowered by my bargain, Master. The figure pointed one of its bony fingers.

"What are you doing?" Azrael's voice was a mixture of anger and fear. "Why can't you just let me be happy?"

Oreth bowed his head. "I am sorry, Azrael. I hope that, when we meet again, you can forgive me."

Azrael began to walk towards the pair, hatred, anger, despair all warring in his face.

"A life, immortal, given." Oreth's eyes filled with tears. *Goodbye, Edison. Goodbye, Liara.*

Azrael's eyes widened as he realized what Oreth was doing. He rushed forward, throwing his power toward Oreth. He said nothing as he tried to stop the sacrifice his enemy was making.

He was too late.

Death's fingers curled into Oreth's chest, passing through flesh and bone to reach the pulsing, beating Alabaster Egg beneath it.

The Egg shattered into splinters under its fingers, and a great green glow suffused the crimson form of the Reaper. The amulet bearing Oreth's name and title shattered with it, the pieces falling into a blackness that appeared below them, a spiritual nothingness that would have chilled the blood of anyone unfortunate enough to see it.

The power, the killing force, which Azrael had sent was sucked into that gaping void. Azrael began to dissolve as well, his soul being pulled out as the magic continued to flow. He screamed, struggling to hold on to his selfhood as he approached Oblivion.

Oreth's eyes shimmered as his soul sought escape. His knees buckled as the vital force began to leave his body, leaving only meat where there once was life. The last thing he saw was a woman, beckoning from behind the trees.

A lightly-tanned woman with dark hair and a radiant smile. A smile that he hadn't seen for millennia.

Eriana was waiting for him, waiting for him to finish what he had to do. He summoned up the remnants of his strength.

"A life...immortal...taken."

The second amulet, bearing Azrael's name and title, shattered as Azrael's body fell to the ground, followed less than a second later by Oreth's.

The bargain is complete.

~~~

Edison and Liara sat at the booth of "their" Denny's, sipping Oreo shakes and coffee.

"Damn fool." Edison bit his lip. "What the fuck was he doing?"
~~~

Liara sighed. "What he thought he had to do." Her gaze lingered on the place where he would have been sitting, were he there.

"Bullshit." Edison dropped his metal cup and it shook the table. "We could have made a better plan, taken more time, come up with something..."

Liara reached across the table, taking Edison's hand in her own. "He wasn't willing to risk it. We had already failed terribly once. We led Azrael to the Matron. That was *our* fault, Edison. *We* did that. *We* got her killed."

Edison's eyes teared up, his mouth struggling to keep the sorrow from escaping, from vocalizing.

"We got *him* killed, you mean." He turned a bit, looking her in the eye. "We weren't smart enough, strong enough, brave enough."

Liara leaned over the table and stared Edison in the face, her deep green eyes commanding his attention.

"We still have to make sure that the new holder of the Nature releases Life and Death from each other's hold." She kissed his hand. "I need you, Edison. We need to finish this work. It's what he wanted from us. His last request."

She held out the letter that Oreth had written to them both; she had found it in Oreth's pocket after the two of them had awoken in the aftermath – Azrael dead, Oreth dead, a scream frozen on one face and a peaceful smile on the other.

"You're right, Liara. It's just difficult...he was more than a friend, I think, at the end, you know? He was family, and I don't remember the last time I really felt like I had family."

Liara sighed. "I know. It's like we just came to know him, and then he was gone. I'm going to miss him too." A small smile crept into the corners of her mouth. "I wonder who got his Nature? Who is the new master of Cities?"

Edison smiled as well. "I don't know, but I'm sure that, whoever he is, he won't be able to replace Oreth, to do as good a job."

"Maybe we should look for him, give him a leg up. I think that Oreth would have wanted that."

"And after that? What happens?"

Liara thought about this, eyes down, finger tapping the table as the server refilled their coffee once again.

"I think I want to write a history of our

kind. Understand who we are. How many. What we've done. That sort of thing. Carve it into Armetium, maybe make a sort of jumping-off place, a school for new Essentials. I don't know." She shrugged. "You?"

Edison paused, stretching out the moment, pretending to consider her question deeply as he rubbed his chin in feigned thought.

"I was thinking that I might work on this school for new Essentials I heard about." He smiled and winked. "I understand that the lady starting it is this really sexy redhead that I might want to get to know better." His smile broadened. "Think she'll take me on?"

Liara leaned in and kissed him. "Anytime, lover mine. Anytime."

The two demigods finished their coffee, left their bill on the table, and boarded a city bus. The driver was a big man, wearing sunglasses and a Hawaiian shirt.

Rob winked and beckoned them aboard.

"Where to?"

EPILOGUE

The ragged woman tucked her children into their beds at the homeless shelter; they were
lucky that they had been able to stay here to-
night, but, as always, there was no guarantee
they would find a spot tomorrow. She hung her
head, her hair drifting down like a curtain over
her face and began to cry, but even her tears
were tired. She had been a good, hard-working
housewife, but her husband had vanished, taking with him everything they had owned. She

had found out, too late, that the house they had lived in together was doomed to foreclosure, and the bank had refused to allow her more time. She had no other skills and no living family to take her in, so she and her children had ended up on the streets, humiliated, hungry, and scared.

Angela, came the whisper, the *demand,* in her mind and in her heart.

Angela's head snapped up, and she wiped her eyes; the voice sounded almost familiar, like someone she had seen recently...but who?

"...Who's there?" Her voice was small, meek, afraid.

I am the Nature, Angela; by joining with me you will live forever. You will have command over all Cities, now and unto eternity. They will be part of you, and you will be part of them. You will never fear death, or want for anything that the City can provide for you ever again.

Angela's hand went to her mouth. Surely, she was going mad. Surely, this was someone playing a trick on her. Surely...

Do you accept, Angela? Will we become one, joining our Natures together to form an

Essential being? Will you become Cities?

Angela licked her lips, and looked over at her children.

Never want, never fear, never again.

She nodded.

"I accept."

END

OTHER NOVELS BY
JASON P. CRAWFORD

CHAINS OF PROPHECY: SAMUEL
BUCKLAND CHRONICLES

SEEKING THE SUN

CYCLES OF DESTRUCTION: EARTH

ABOUT THE AUTHOR

Jason Patrick Crawford is a father of three rambunctious boys and has been happily married for almost 10 years. He first cut his literary "chops" as a storyteller in various roleplaying games, ranging from Dungeons and Dragons to the White Wolf system and Nobilis. Jason hails from Louisiana but has traveled many places - first as an 'army brat' and then while serving as a linguist in the United States Army for six years. He now teaches high school chemistry, biology and physics in the California desert. While Jason Patrick Crawford wears many hats well, he has found his calling and his passion in writing novels.

Connect with Me Online:

My Website:
http://www.jasonpatrickcrawford.com
My Blog:
http://jasonpatrickcrawford.blogspot.com/
My Smashwords:
https://www.smashwords.com/profile/view/
jasoncrawford
Facebook: https://www.facebook.com/
JasonPatrickCrawford
Twitter:
@jnewmanwriting
My Email:
jasonpatrickcrawford@epitomepress.com

Please consider leaving a review if you en-
joyed this book. Independent authors thrive on
the feedback of our readers, and I would love to
know what you thought!